The Ceremony
of Innocence

Also by Jamake Highwater

FICTION
The Sun, He Dies
Anpao
Journey to the Sky
Legend Days
Eyes of Darkness

POETRY
Moonsong Lullaby

NONFICTION
Many Smokes, Many Moons: *A Chronology of American Indian History Through Indian Art*

Dance: *Rituals of Experience*

Ritual of the Wind: *North American Indian Ceremonies, Music and Dance*

Song from the Earth: *North American Indian Painting*

Indian America: *A Cultural and Travel Guide*

The Sweet Grass Lives On: *Fifty Contemporary North American Indian Artists*

The Primal Mind: *Vision and Reality in Indian America*

Masterpieces of Indian Painting (8 folios)

Arts of the Indian Americas: *Leaves from the Sacred Tree*

Words in the Blood: *An Anthology of Contemporary Native American Literature* (editor)

The Ceremony of Innocence

JAMAKE HIGHWATER

Harper & Row, Publishers

TO MARION
For an opera
performance that has lasted a lifetime!

Library of Congress Cataloging in Publication Data
Highwater, Jamake.
    The ceremony of innocence.

    (Pt. two of the Ghost horse cycle)
    "A Charlotte Zolotow book."
    Summary: Alone and destitute after the death of her
husband, Amana finds friendship, love and finally
disillusionment when she strives to give her daughter
and grandchildren a sense of pride in their Indian
heritage.
    1. Indians of North America—Juvenile fiction.
[1. Indians of North America—Fiction]   1. Title.
II. Series: Highwater, Jamake. Ghost horse cycle ;
pt. 2.
PZ7.H5443Ce 1985   [Fic]   84-48334
ISBN 0-06-022301-4
ISBN 0-06-022302-2 (lib. bdg.)

Designed by Barbara A. Fitzsimmons
10 9 8 7 6 5 4 3 2 1
First Edition

Turning and turning in the widening gyre
The falcon cannot hear the falconer;
Things fall apart; the center cannot hold;
Mere anarchy is loosed upon the world,
The blood-dimmed tide is loosed, and everywhere
The ceremony of innocence is drowned;
The best lack all conviction, while the worst
Are full of passionate intensity.

W. B. Yeats

PART
I

FAUST: *The Mothers! Mothers!*
…a strange word is said!

GOETHE

ONE

It was in the winter that Amana found a friend.

The days were filled with gusty blue air . . . with soot and dust. The bruised gray mud of the street froze into deep rippling wounds on which Amana slipped and fell as she thrust herself against the wind and followed a silent group of forlorn Indians toward the trading post.

She was begging among the white men when she heard laughter. It was a sound so filled with defiance that it roused in Amana a sense of freedom she had not felt since the death of her husband, Far Away Son, three years ago.

"I don't want no more French mans," a woman was shouting at a white man. "And I don't want no Injun neither. No Englis and no Injun. And not you neither, fat man! I don't want any mans! You hear me good!" And then she laughed and her laughter filled the whole valley. It reached through the ferocious grief that had lived inside Amana since the death of Far Away Son.

The white man pulled back as if he had been struck. He turned toward his friends, who grinned. The woman was one of the French-Cree half-breeds from Red River.

"How daring for you to treat me like whore!" she shouted at the man as he fled. "How daring for you!"

"Just look at that hag!" a man said, pushing Amana's begging hands out of his way. "Just take a look at that half-breed bitch!" He glared at the Cree woman. "It's the way all of them act . . . as if they were something special. All they are is filth! For one thing, they eat dogs. And they're the worst pack of cheats and liars that ever traveled across the plains! She acts like she's as good as us, but she's just an old whore!"

The Indian woman whirled around and strode in his direction.

"What you call me?" she muttered into the man's face. "*Putain!* . . . Whore! Is that what you are calling me?" she shouted. "That is what they all calling for me! For them doing it . . . that fine thing. But when I am going with any them . . . me *putain!*" She spat on the ground in front of him. "I spit!" she hissed. "I spit between your legs, mister! Ha! You think women die for having you! But I just laughing for you!" She put her hands on her wide hips and burst into derisive laughter. "*Oui, mon cher*, we just laughing for you!"

The man backed away, and as the woman glared from side to side, the other men moved out of her path.

She laughed even louder than before as she trudged forward, dragging a sack of weathered bones, skulls, and antlers into the trading post. "Hey, *ma chère*," she said with a wide smile as she noticed Amana, "maybe you give little help for me."

Amana looked into the painted face of the woman. Without speaking, she reached for an edge of the heavy sack and helped the woman drag her burden up the muddy steps and into the sweet, warm smoke that radiated from the glowing stove of the trading post.

"Hey you, traderman," the woman yelled fiercely.

"Okay, okay, Amalia," the trader grunted, nodding with a resigned expression. "Just hold your horses and I'll be there. Got other things to do, y'know, besides fuss over you."

The woman laughed again. "If I act like lady, what getting it for me, huh?" she said to Amana with a smile. "Better I make big noise and scare this stinking traderman not for cheating me all time!" she exclaimed. "You see," she muttered as the trader strolled toward them, "this bastard know I ain't doing no kidding round. He know not cheat Amalia or there is big troubles."

After the trader and Amalia briefly haggled over the price for her sack of bones, she selected the goods she wanted in exchange for her harvest of skulls and antlers, insisting upon a few items beyond those the trader was willing to give her.

"Okay, okay, Amalia," he said, "take the damn sugar and all the rest of it and get on your way before you scare off all my customers."

"You betcha I scare good." Amalia laughed. "Me and my friend here," she said, throwing her arm around Amana's waist, "we going have pretty *magnifique dîner*! That for sure!"

After the two women had packed their provisions into Amalia's green wagon, Amana gazed at her new friend, uncertain if she was just drunk or if she truly meant to share her food and shelter. There had been so many disappointments, so much pain and hunger, since Amana's husband had been trampled to death in a buffalo hunt. She had been alone, without family or friends. It was only her dreams that gave her the courage to survive. She awakened each day with the torment of her empty stomach, but she never failed to dream herself back into existence. And sometimes she sang the powerful spirit song of the foxes, the song that had been given to her in her childhood.

"Aih," Amalia sighed gently, touching Amana's shoulder. "Why you so sad all suddenly? Come on, my friend, we need being much happy for each other sake. Too much *malheur* . . . too many sadness already in world." Then, in a gruff voice, she added, "I work too hard all time, so you maybe drive wagon." Slowly, she scanned the crowd of curious onlookers in front of the trading post, scowling and flicking her thumb over her teeth at them. "What you foolish staring for!" she exclaimed. "Got nothing better for doing?"

Amana climbed into the driver's seat while Amalia sat in the back of the open wagon, dangling her long legs into the dust as they turned out toward the open plain. They rattled along gracelessly. Amalia jostled to and fro in a delighted drunken stupor, singing and tilting a whiskey flask to her mouth.

One good day Coyote
walking down the path.
One day old Coyote
meeting with a pretty woman.
"What you have there
in your pack?"
she asked Coyote.
"Fish eggs I have,"
said old Coyote with a smirk.
"And can I have some to eat?"
the pretty woman, she asked.
So old Coyote, he say,
"If you close your eyes and
hold up your dress!"
HA!

Amalia's father had been a white hunter from Montreal. Her husband had been French. Amalia told Amana all about the good life of the forest before her husband had died. Amana recalled the day she had come across two survivors of her tribe: the grandmothers called Weasel Woman and Crow Woman. Eventually she had been reunited with her invalid sister, SoodaWa.

"It was a terrible day when my elder sister SoodaWa died," Amana murmured. "Then I was alone with the old man named Far Away Son who was husband to both of us. But I came to love him because he was strong in his heart and loyal. And he let me ride with him and hunt and go on raiding parties. And we were happy . . . until the day that he died."

Amana and Amalia shared the stories of their lives as they rattled over the plains toward Amalia's house. Both women still mourned their husbands. Amalia's man had been killed in a hunting accident when they lived with the French-Cree in Canada. He had been killed just as Far Away Son had died—trampled by stampeding buffalo. Both women had been left on their own, wandering from camp to camp and trading post to trading post without friends or relatives. Amalia had no family; and all of Amana's people had died from the terrible sickness or during the starvation years.

"Amana et Amalia!" the Cree woman exclaimed. "Amalia and Amana! What good luck names we are! We be the inseparables. *Oui, ma chère? Inséparables!"*

* * *

Amalia's house was made of sod and large branches, and it was warm. The land around the cabin was inert and gray, as if it had died of a long and painful illness. Though the large game had vanished from the region, Amana still managed to snare rabbits and grouse. She knew how to raid the nests of mice for lily roots. And she knew how to hunt the eggs of wild birds. These meager rations kept the women alive during the hard days. But getting money to buy the provisions that only the trading post provided was far more difficult than foraging for food. Amana was strong and she understood how to find the gifts that the land provided, but she understood nothing about dollars.

Amalia, however, knew all about the white man's

money. She traveled around the prairie in the battered green wagon she had inherited from her French husband, and she collected the dried bones of animals. For many days she scoured the plains for skulls and bones that lay buried in the dead grass.

"They making them into much things," Amalia explained to Amana. "Gunpowder is making from these bones . . . and *l'engrais*, you know, what you say . . . fertilizer. *Oui?*"

With the money they received for the bones they bought meat and flour to make bannock bread, and if there was enough money left they purchased tea, sugar, and lard. Then they bought some whiskey for Amalia.

"This *alcool* only thing keeping poor Amalia living," she told Amana apologetically. "I sorry, *ma chère*, spending hard money for the bad whiskey, but this only thing keeping me living."

Amana embraced her. "Never mind, Amalia," she said. "I love you."

Amalia's eyes filled with tears, and she turned away. Amana smiled and then nodded with grief. It was her twenty-eighth winter, and all the days were bad. It was hard to be alive.

There were not enough buffalo chips on the plains with which to build a fire, and there was no food. So Amalia took the green wagon and went off to Fort Benton, where the white men gave her food and money for staying with them. Amana lay awake, shivering and gasping frosty breaths as she listened to the lonely sound of the crickets in the corners of the empty cabin. She tried to summon the comforting faces of her sister, SoodaWa, and her husband, Far Away Son, but their images, like the days of their lives, had vanished. So many people had disappeared, and so much had happened to Amana, that her memory had become scarred like an old wound that would not heal. And the wound hurt.

Her own people had abandoned Amana—that memory would never leave her in peace. It haunted her like a long shrill noise that resounded through the night. And in the mornings she awakened exhausted. She dreamed about the angry hunters who had blamed her for the death of Far Away Son. "If you had been content to be like other women and stayed home," they had said, "your husband would still be alive. If you had been a woman instead of a warrior, a wife instead of a hunter . . . Far Away Son would still be with us."

Amana groaned. None of the men of her tribe had spoken on her behalf. No one had befriended her. And so Amana had been turned away, while the women had cried out to her, begging her to forgive their husbands and sons, asking her to bless them with her power.

Amana threw back her head in agony—so cruel was the recollection of the scandal that had surrounded her. She would not beg for the loyalty of those men she had helped to feed during the days of starvation. And yet no one would speak in her defense. No one opened his lodge to her. And finally one morning she was left

in a circle of dust and debris as the horse
pulled endlessly away, gliding into the unbroken u.
tion that now surrounded her. Now nothing remained
but this empty cabin where she lay sleepless, with the
moon hiding among the dark trees in shame.

Amana peered out into the black land, searching for
some small sign of life. But there was only the dark
wall of night everywhere.

*   *   *

Amana loved Amalia and missed her, yet she did not
truly understand her. Amalia's strength was violent, unlike the gentle power of holy people. She wasn't a warrior but something new and different and frighten-
ing . . . something that Amana herself could never become. Amalia's courage was born of arrogance and
anger. Amana watched her with a mixture of admiration
and dread: her daring and rancor, her defiance and the
rich, violent rage that poured from her like rifle shots
bursting in the air. Warrior though she had been, Amana
could not find Amalia's sort of fierceness within herself.
She felt useless and weak.

She could not be a warrior in the strange new land
surrounding Fort Benton. All dreams of power dried
up and died there. The voices of storytellers became
silent. Their tales of destiny fell like leaves in an endless
autumn. The powerful animals withdrew into the distant
land where white men had not found their way, taking
with them the wisdom they had once shared with Indians. The animals would not speak to people any longer.

They had run away to a place beyond the reach of men.

For an Indian woman alone there seemed no choice except to beg or to sleep with strangers. There was no other way to survive. She would have died in the first lonely winter had she not walked for six days to this place where the white people had built their houses of mud and soot and wood. There the drunks, the outcasts, the widows, the children, the old ones, the deformed, and the sick could plead to the white man for pennies.

"*Aih* . . . help me," Amana whimpered in the darkness of the cabin, tears turning to ice upon her cheeks.

She reached out into the darkness and moved her hands in the air, trying to summon the past for comfort and strength. The crickets fell silent. The cold air stung her. Gently, she placed her fingers on the medicine bundle hidden beside her bed, whispering to it, conjuring it into life, begging it for a song that would give her courage. But the power was gone. The bundle did not answer.

*   *   *

Amalia did not return for many days. Amana waited anxiously, fearing that perhaps she had been killed or that she had been thrown into jail or had simply gone off with somebody. When Amalia finally came home, Amana wept with relief as her friend pranced drunkenly into the cabin with her arms filled with good things to eat, and some bright-red cloth for a new dress.

"*Ma chère!*" she bawled. "You getting new dress what I making like perfect from Paris! *Très élégante, ma chère, trèèèès élégante!* And after that we going for *la grande danse des Assiniboins! Oui?*—you know what I saying for you, *ma chère?* The dance you calling *As-sin-ah-pes-ka!*"

Amana was so pleased to see Amalia that she agreed to go to the dance.

"Ah! . . . *Que c'est charmant!* . . . How nice!" Amalia exclaimed with enthusiasm, when she unwrapped the red cloth and waved it in the air. "Maybe for once time you do what your Amalia tells best for you, *oui?* What a new dress this is being soon! *Que c'est belle!* . . . How beautiful, *ma chère!*"

"I'm not beautiful and I go to the dance only for you," Amana insisted as Amalia playfully draped the red fabric around her friend's shoulders.

"*Que c'est belle!*" she insisted. "With a new dress and maybe little *très* smart *coiffure* . . . with some pretty paint for the lips and"—Amalia stood back and studied Amana with deep concentration—"and *voilà, ma chère*, you being new womans! *Que c'est belle!* . . . *Vraiment, que c'est très belle!*"

Amana smiled tolerantly as Amalia fussed over her, but she pulled away when her friend lifted the scissors to her long black hair. "No!" she exclaimed. "Amalia, no!"

"But *ma chère* . . ."

"No," Amana repeated gently. "I will let you put me in a white woman's dress and I will go to the dance, but I will not let you cut my hair."

"Ah, *quel dommage!* . . . Such a pity," Amalia sighed.

"And no paint on my lips . . ."

"*Ridicule*," Amalia pouted. Then her stern, disapproving expression turned into a wide smile and she embraced Amana. "Ah, some good time we going for tonight, Amana!"

* * *

When Amana and Amalia reached Fort Benton, they found that there were perhaps three thousand Indians who had come down from Canada and across from the plains to barter with the white men of the trading post. By comparison with the Indians living at Fort Benton, these visitors were sturdy and handsome. Amana gazed at them with longing, wishing that she might ride away with them back into the open land that lay to the north. But the nomads looked past her, having no use for Indian women dressed in the clothes of the white man.

Hoping to find someone she knew from long ago, Amana peered into the faces, but she recognized no one. Many of the men were already drunk, and those who were still sober strolled in wide circles as they talked to old friends they had not seen since the last gathering of the tribes.

Then, as the drums began to call to one another, the dancing began.

"Don't worries," Amalia assured Amana as they worked their way through the crowd. "These fellas not bother nobody, believing me, *ma chère.*"

As it grew dark, a great fire was built in the dance circle and the old women, wrapped in Hudson's Bay blankets, nodded their heads happily as they moved with small steps to the beating of the drums. Then the young people, dressed in their finest clothes, began to assemble for the Assiniboin dance.

Only the younger, unmarried men and women were allowed to take part. The elders sang and watched as the singing resounded across the little valley.

"Come on, Amana," Amalia exclaimed, "we go do some dancing too!"

But Amana was too embarrassed to join the dancers in their handsome buckskin dresses. They stared at her European dress and her red sash with disapproval.

The Indian girls stood on one side of the dance circle while the young men lined up on the other side. They took small steps forward, coming closer and closer to one another, singing loudly and looking into each other's eyes.

While Amalia talked to a tall, bearded man, Amana watched the young people. How lovely they were and how good it was after so many months in Fort Benton to see people dressed in their beautiful regalia and holding themselves with pride and elegance!

"Hey, *ma chère*," Amalia called. "*Je vous en prie . . .* do not sit there all for yourself. Come dancing!"

Amana blushed when people turned to see who was making so much noise. But Amalia was oblivious to the stares and continued calling in her great booming voice, "Come dancing!"

Amana backed out of the bright firelight and waved

her friend away again and again. Among white men it was humorous for Amalia to shout and to play the crazy Indian, but among these traditional people such behavior was mortifying. Everyone stared and whispered. It was shameful to be so loud at a gathering of Indians. And Amana hated to be ashamed of her dearest friend.

Finally Amalia shrugged and rejoined the exuberant dancers, leaving Amana in peace.

The darkness beyond the firelight was cool and comforting. Amana wanted to dance; she wanted to talk to people and to laugh, but a deep winter had invaded her and frozen her heart. The warrior in her breast slept his deep sleep. And the woman in Amana was lost in an endless blizzard of wind and snow, a vast world in which she could not find her way.

Then there was a sound.

Amana turned and faced the unbroken darkness of the prairie that stretched out beyond the dance circle. The voices of the dancers receded, and the campfire sailed away and released the black power of the night.

"*Aih,*" whimpered Amana.

She crouched close to the earth and began to tremble. Something was creeping slowly toward her.

In the distance, dim and deadly, stood a huge owl. He blinked his yellow eyes. He placed his large hands upon his groin and smiled at Amana. "Come with me," he said. "I want you."

Suddenly the campfire circle lurched, throwing up a crimson flurry of sparks. When the smoke cleared, the owl had vanished, leaving only a glistening red shadow hanging motionless in the air.

"*Mon Dieu!* . . . You cold like death, *chère amie!*" Amalia was saying as she embraced her friend. "What is matter for you? Why you here in dark? Why you not come dancing? The mans like you even best than for me! *Oui!*"

Amana trembled and leaned into her friend's arms, frightened and tired. She felt plain and useless and afraid.

"Come . . . coming back near fire, *ma chère*. Come where people can see how you pretty. Come, *amie.*"

But Amana was confused and ashamed. The omen of the owl lingered in her mind . . . a dreadful dream she had not had since she was a child, when the owls tried to destroy her and the foxes rescued her from their powers.

"Come near fire, *ma chère*," Amalia urged gently, leading Amana into the light. "What happen for you, Amana?"

Amana could not speak. She glanced back over her shoulder into the darkness. Then, as the light surrounded her, she shriveled and felt exhausted. She did not know how to walk in the dress Amalia had made for her, or how to sit down. Her self-consciousness grew unbearable as young Indian women glanced at her.

Then a man suddenly touched her shoulder. "*Mademoiselle?*"

Amana looked at him blankly.

"Ah," Amalia sighed. "So I find out you knowing already this Jean-Pierre Bonneville."

"Yes . . ." Amana stammered. "Yes . . . that's right. I met you at the trading post. Long ago . . . when I came with Far Away Son. Yes, I recall." And Amana smiled at the tall man, who was gazing at her warmly. "Yes . . . I know you," she whispered, grateful for his friendliness among so many strangers.

"Well," Amalia interrupted with a grin, "good you know this Jean-Pierre Bonneville. He having too good looks like a sweetheart!"

"You brought some skins to my trading post," the man said to Amana with a bright smile.

"Yes, that's right. That was so long ago," Amana murmured, looking away self-consciously.

In the awkward silence Bonneville continued to gaze at Amana.

"Well, Amalia, the dance is over," Amana said abruptly, "and it is almost morning. Maybe we should start for home."

"Home . . . home . . . home . . ." Amalia muttered. "Such marvelous dancing and all you saying is *bonsoir. . . .*"

"We must go," Amana insisted.

"I'll help you get her into the wagon," Bonneville said as he supported Amalia, who had had too much to drink.

"*Zut! Zut!*" Amalia muttered as she climbed into the back of the wagon box, where she could lie down.

"I'm sorry," Amana whispered. "My friend drinks too much whiskey."

"It's a pleasure to help you, *mademoiselle*," he said.

Amana could not look at him. "It is almost morning," she said flatly. "Good night."

But when the wagon lurched into the blackness, Amana glanced back over her shoulder. Jean-Pierre Bonneville stood in the bright light watching them. His body was carved out of the darkness by the blast of the dance fire that blazed behind him. But then the wagon descended into a valley, and the glistening apparition faded into the wide deep night of the prairie.

*   *   *

Amana did not see Jean-Pierre Bonneville for many weeks. And yet the image of his body cast against the great bonfire filled her dreams, comforting her. There was something about him unlike any man Amana had known. He was not like an Indian, but he was not the same as the other white men. She did not understand Jean-Pierre Bonneville. Yet she hoped she might see him again.

"What you thinking for now?" Amalia would ask with a wise grin. "You look like womans with some kinda fella in her head." And then she would laugh and gaily prance around the cabin, lifting her dress over her head outrageously, playing the clown until Amana could not restrain her laughter. "Ah-ha!" Amalia exclaimed. "Maybe we get for Amana a boysfriend yet!"

"Hush!" Amana said. "All you think about is men and love!"

Yet Amana *was* thinking of Jean-Pierre Bonneville, and she could not find the courage to admit to Amalia how she felt about him.

"Well, maybe for you it is good time to be here . . .
way far out in the nothing. But for me there is too
much nothing!" Amalia grumbled, stopping her dance
and sitting dejectedly on her mattress of straw. "Maybe
you not like thinking for the mans, but for me I want
some dancing and fun!"

They had a small bundle of rabbit skins to barter,
so the two women decided to return to the trading post.

"We will go tomorrow?" Amana asked when Amalia
suggested it was time to sell the pelts. "When will we
go?"

"I think maybe *demain* we go for trading post, *oui.*"

Amalia was busy counting the furs and didn't notice
her friend's bright smile. Amana wondered about her
intense happiness. She would see Jean-Pierre Bonneville
again! She felt absurd and marvelous at the same time.

He was so eloquent and gentle. He was so handsome.
"Ma-che-ye-num!" she murmured. That Blackfeet word
echoed like drumming back through all the bad days,
to a sweet summer night when her husband Far Away
Son and the grandmothers sat under the immense skele-
ton of a cottonwood tree, and her friend Yellow Bird
Woman confided a secret plan to elope with a handsome
young man. Was it possible that Amana now felt the
burning love her friend had described on that long-ago
summer's night . . . a night filled with fireflies that tumbled like blazing snow through the wide leafless boughs
of the old cottonwood tree?

Amana lay awake with a singing heart. Her fingers
slowly moved over her cheeks and lips. Was she at all

handsome? Her fingers questioned each bone of her face and each lock of her hair, but she could not find an answer. She had never paid any attention to her appearance. Now she wanted to creep from her mat and peek into Amalia's looking glass by candlelight. But she lay in the darkness gazing into the handsome face of Jean-Pierre Bonneville, which she conjured in the air.

Was she attractive enough for him? Did he truly think she was pretty?

In the morning Amana awakened singing and hurried to help make breakfast and to pack the wagon for the trip.

"I think maybe you got something on mind asides rabbit skins, *ma chère*!" Amalia laughed as she heaved the pelts into the wagon and climbed on top of them.

"Hush, Amalia," Amana exclaimed as she urged the horse forward and the wagon lumbered over the prairie-dog mounds and rattled toward the trading post.

"Never do I see someone so shy like you, Amana," her friend said gently. "Never I see such thing like you."

"I'm not shy and I'm not in love!"

"Oh"—Amalia laughed—"nobody say nothing for love! From you, *ma chère*, first time I hear about this things!"

"Well," Amana insisted, "I'm not shy! If you had seen me in the days when I went on war parties with Far Away Son, you would know that I am not shy!"

And yet, no sooner had Amana gotten to the trading post than she was overwhelmed by a sense of plainness and crushed with embarrassment at the prospect of seeing Jean-Pierre Bonneville.

"What for matter with you?" Amalia complained when Amana fell silent.

"I'll stay in the wagon and wait for you," Amana said, averting her eyes.

"Ah, what a foolish!" Amalia huffed with exasperation. "Sometime I think maybe you crazy woman. You want to stay in wagon . . . so stay!"

While Amalia was selling the skins and packing the provisions in the wagon, Jean-Pierre came to the door and smiled at Amana. Amana could not look at him.

"Hello again," he said in a soft voice as he came out into the afternoon sunlight, his hair turning amber and yellow as he walked. "I have something for you," he murmured, pressing a silk handkerchief into Amana's palm.

Amalia did not see Jean-Pierre's gift. She grunted as she climbed into the wagon. *"Hey-ho!"* she shouted to the horse in her big voice. And then she glanced with the expression of amusement and contempt with which she usually regarded men, and said, *"Bonsoir,* Jean-Pierre Bonneville . . . and be a good fellow for change! *Bonsoir!"*

Amana and Jean-Pierre looked with intense longing at one another. Amana crushed the handkerchief to her breast and the wagon abruptly drew them apart.

"Bonsoir . . ." he whispered.

* * *

The next time Amalia and Amana came to the trading post for provisions, there was a dance being held for some French people who had come from their distant land over the ocean to purchase furs from the Indians. There was a great deal of singing and drinking and loud talking, and Amalia, who loved the noise and gaiety, refused to return home until she had visited the large cabin where the dance was being held.

"Bonsoir, bonsoir . . . entrez, mes demoiselles; entrez, s'il vous plaît!" a drunken white man cooed to Amana and Amalia. ". . . Come on in, young ladies; come in!"

Amana ignored the grin on the man's whiskered face. He was the partner of Jean-Pierre Bonneville—the same man who, when Amana had visited the trading post four summers earlier, had followed her into a cottonwood grove in an attempt to rape her. She recognized him with repulsion.

"Oh, *ma chère*, he not such terrible mans. It just his hands what is terrible bad!" Amalia laughed and cuffed the man on the shoulder.

He grinned, gazing at Amana as if he enjoyed embarrassing her.

Amana could not understand how Jean-Pierre and this vulgar man could be partners—one so gentle and polite and the other so crude and aggressive.

"I want to leave," Amana murmured to Amalia.

"*Chérie*. . . please! Relax for yourself and take a good time for once," Amalia entreated, grasping Amana by the wrist.

"Ki-tak-stai pes-ka?" someone whispered to Amana just as she broke free of Amalia's strong grasp and was about to flee from the noisy cabin.

"Ki-tak-stai pes-ka? . . . Will you dance?" the man asked again.

It was Jean-Pierre Bonneville.

Amana was delighted to hear him speak her language.

"Aih . . . yes," she stammered. She glanced around the room as she extended her arm toward Jean-Pierre.

He led her to the center of the floor. Another quadrille was being formed. Amana drew a faltering breath, uncertain if she could do this kind of dancing . . . hoping she might be graceful and that she would find courage to return the open smile with which Jean-Pierre Bonneville coaxed her into the crowd.

"Come along, my friend," he said softly. "We will make our own dance circle and all the other people will disappear."

And then as drums and fiddles made their thumping, screeching music, they began to dance.

Amana stumbled. She tried again. She smiled shyly. He tossed his head of thick black hair. And soon they were moving across the floor like birds in a windy sky.

When the dance was over, Amana became aware of other people crowded around them. She tugged anxiously at Bonneville's hand, hoping to leave the center of the floor. She felt very conspicuous. But Jean-Pierre would not let her go.

"Please stay and talk," he said quietly. He smiled to reassure her.

"I am not good at talking," Amana murmured, looking down.

"But you are doing just fine," he insisted gently.

Amana wanted to stay with him. She wanted to look at him. But the bad days, the starvation days, the years of death and wandering, had destroyed her pride in herself. She felt buried deep within her own body.

"I must go . . ." she stammered, glancing into his face and feeling awkward and unwomanly. "I must go . . . Amalia is looking for me," she said. She turned away. She wanted to remain with him and dance to the strange tinny music, but she felt increasingly uneasy and so self-conscious that she could not bear being near him.

Jean-Pierre laughed as if she were joking with him. "But Amalia never wants to go and she never looks for anybody," he teased.

"Amalia is my friend!" Amana said, her dark eyes flashing. Her humiliation suddenly turned to rage. "I must go now!" she exclaimed fiercely.

"But why are you angry and why are you in such a hurry? You haven't even told me your name."

"I don't like standing here in the middle of the room. It is ridiculous to stand here like this, with everyone listening to us. It's ridiculous and I want to go."

"But why?"

"Because," she snapped, "everyone is staring at me!"

"Well, of course everybody is looking at you. You're very beautiful. . . . Naturally people like to look at you. Don't you realize how beautiful you are?"

Amana felt that he was making a fool of her. She

wanted to strike him. She felt like lashing out and hitting him across his face. "You are making fun of me!" she muttered, pulling her wrist from his grasp. "I will not be insulted by you or by anyone else! I am not beautiful and I know it very well! I am full of bad days and bad nights. I am nothing and I have nothing, but I will not let you humiliate me! Good night, Jean-Pierre Bonneville!"

Amana fled from the cabin and ran into the darkness, where she began to tremble and to weep.

"Jean-Pierre," she murmured. "Now I have lost you."

*   *   *

Amana waited all night for Amalia to return to the wagon. When she finally did arrive, she was drunk and loud, and she was irritable.

"Damn mans!" she growled as she flopped into the back of the wagon. "They no-good liars! Damn mans!"

Before Amana could reply, Amalia rolled over and began to snore.

Amana silently climbed into the driver's seat, feeling lonely and forlorn. Already it was dawn. The sun was making its red beadwork along the black neckline of the land, sending scarlet birds into the dark sky. Amana prodded the horse toward home, then released the reins and let the animal find its own way across the golden grass. She took a deep breath and tilted back her head, gazing upward with equal amazement for the vastness of the brightening sky and the magnitude of feelings that spread within her like a prairie fire.

*   *   *

Amana could not stop thinking about Jean-Pierre Bonneville. She tried to force him from her mind. But his perfect face reappeared, and she would be lost in the echo of the music to which they had danced. She would be lost in his smile. Sometimes in the evening, when Amalia went to Fort Benton, Amana would clutch the small fragment of looking glass on Amalia's table and explore the dark face she found within the mirror. Was she attractive? Was it possible? Perhaps it was true. . . . Maybe there was some small trace of beauty. She wondered if Jean-Pierre Bonneville could truly see something in her face that she did not see. If so, she had been unfair to him.

With these troubled thoughts Amana walked out into the black landscape and raised her arms toward the stars that blistered the immense darkness. She felt a loneliness she had not felt before: a hunger in her limbs more consuming than the hunger of the winters of starvation.

Over the weeks, Amana realized she no longer feared Jean-Pierre Bonneville. He was not like other white men. That look of admiration in his eyes made Amana proud—it even made her feel beautiful.

And so one morning, when Amana went out into the cold air to fetch water from the creek, she smiled with delight to see Jean-Pierre dismounting and slowly walking toward her.

Courting a woman by the watering place was an ancient custom, and Amana was deeply touched that a white man would honor her in the old ways. She smiled at him and allowed him to place his fingers upon her shoulder as he gazed into her face.

He said nothing. He only looked at her. Then he went silently away.

As the days passed, Jean-Pierre often came to see Amana, secretly meeting her by the watering place. Each time he would bring her a present. And then they would walk silently into the open mouth of the night.

Amana cautioned Jean-Pierre not to visit when Amalia was at home.

"She will be angry," she whispered.

When he objected, she insisted, and he fell silent, accepting what Amana said.

And so whenever Amalia went off to Fort Benton to have a good time for a few days, Amana and Jean-Pierre would spend the long night strolling without direction. Touching, looking at one another, smiling but rarely speaking. And in the morning, as soon as the sky became light, Amana would send him away, fearful that Amalia might come home unexpectedly.

"But why are you afraid of Amalia?" he asked.

"Because I have made people angry at me before," she exclaimed.

"If you feel that way about Amalia, then you must not live here. You must come live with me," he said when he was leaving.

Then they both laughed. Their laughter stretched like a cloud across the white morning, and then broke into silence as Jean-Pierre galloped away and disappeared.

*   *   *

He promised to be kind to her. And he promised never to abandon her. He won her with his gentle words and his smiling eyes. Like two animals dancing in circles in an open field, they had come to know one another by smell and touch and color. She had come to Jean-Pierre Bonneville and he had come to her. And so one day Amana admitted to Amalia that she thought Jean-Pierre Bonneville was a very good man.

"Jamais!" Amalia huffed. "He never being a real mans! You silly girl." She laughed bitterly as she flicked her thumb against her front teeth in a gesture of contempt. *"Fille! Vieille fille!"*

"But, Amalia, I think I like him," Amana said quietly.

"Pooh! You are liking him, *ma chère,* 'cause he make you feel strong. *N'est-ce pas?* For cause he no real mans! Believing for your friend, *ma chère.* He no good for you. 'Cause these white mans, they no like him neither. Believing what your Amalia is telling for you, *ma chère.* The white mans, they calling him *garçonnet*—little boy. That is what his own mans calling for him. Ha! . . . They all time laughing for him!"

"No, Amalia, you are not fair to him," Amana said softly. "I know something about him, and believe me, he is a good man." She sat in front of the fireplace and looked into the flames. "He is nice to me. He gives me presents, and he's gentle and good."

"You never tell me this. What for you keeping secrets from your Amalia? What secrets are these? What he bringing for you, Amana?"

"All kinds of things . . . necklaces and a brooch with

a little woman's face on it. A green ribbon. A handkerchief. That was the first thing he ever gave me—a silk
handkerchief. Here, let me show it to you. It's so pretty!''

And with a smile Amana drew the handkerchief from
her bodice.

"Merde!" Amalia suddenly shouted as she slashed the
air with her hand and turned away from Amana. Then
she whirled around as if to speak, but instead she laughed
loudly and clenched her hands on her hips. *"En voilà
assez!*. . . Enough for all this nonsense! *Assez, ma chère.*
What caring for us about this stupid white pig Jean-Pierre
Bonneville? This pig of a white mans! Come here giving
your Amalia a big kiss and maybe we make *dîner magnifique* of too much rabbits and whiskey and lots good thing
and we forget all about this *ridicule* white man. *Oui?"*

"But I like him, Amalia. I truly like him," Amana
repeated resolutely. "He is the first young man I have
ever really liked.''

"Ah," Amalia muttered. She frowned as she sat down
slowly. She sighed with exhaustion. "So you liking
for him like that, huh. *Maintenant, maintenant je com-
prends* . . . yes, I understood you now, *ma chère.''*

Amalia grinned bitterly, an expression of disdain
flooding her face.

"So," she said drily, "maybe now somedays sooner
or lately he ask for you coming his house. *Oui, chez
lui* . . . *n'est-ce pas?* And then Amalia and Amana
finish . . . *finis* . . . no more friends.''

Amana glanced away.

"You hid this from your good friend," Amalia whispered. "*Merde, comme c'est triste* . . . how sad it is that friends like you and me keep secrets about something so full with happiness."

Then suddenly Amalia began to weep. She turned her head sharply away and a long groan came from her chest.

It was the first time Amana had ever seen her friend weep.

"Amalia," Amana murmured as she touched Amalia's shoulder. "I should have told you, but I was afraid. I know I should have told you about this . . . but I couldn't say anything."

Amalia would not look at Amana.

"Amalia," Amana whispered, "we will always be friends. I owe you everything, Amalia—yes, it is true; I owe you my life. I don't forget! If it were not for your help, I would still be begging for coins at Fort Benton."

"*Ah, merde!*" Amalia muttered, pushing away her tears and shrugging like a man. "No pity, *s'il vous plaît!* Amalia not need your pity or grateful talk neither. I knew it all time. The mans, they call me whore! Ha! They never nice for me. But now you get mans right away! Sure, right away Amana get everything and Amalia get nothing. You get this *fille*! This *garçonnet*! And I get nothing. You see how stupid is this crazy life? *Merde!*"

Amana looked away in pain. She did not know what to say. Then she rose quickly and went to the door, pausing in the hope that one of them might have words to help. The silence was suffocating.

"Amalia," Amana said slowly, leaning heavily against the door. She turned to face her friend. Amalia was glaring at her with unclouded rage. "Long ago I put away my dreams and I put aside my most precious visions, and I married an old man. I took care of my elder sister and I provided for my grandmothers. But gradually, by doing things for other people, I lost my own reason for living. Then I lost my only sister. And I lost my husband, Far Away Son. And I lost my people. I am not an Indian anymore, Amalia, and I have not learned how to be anyone else. I have not learned how to fight and yet I have not learned how to give up."

Then Amana wept with the pain that filled her. "I love you, Amalia. I say again, I owe you everything— even my life. But that is not enough to keep me alive. I can't give myself up again for the sake of those I love. I must have a reason of my own to live."

Then Amana quickly closed the door behind her.

T W O

On white moonlit nights they slept on the edge of a
high-cut bank near the river. It was deep summer, and
the heat loomed just above the luminous earth. One
night, when everything was intensely defined and real,
they watched as the moonlight lingered tangibly in the
humid air. The turbulent river seemed strangely motionless.

A spider twisted on its glowing thread, dangling up-
side down and slowly moving its long back legs in an
endless succession of meticulous gestures, conjuring silver out of nothing.

An owl hooted in the distance, and Amana trembled.

"What's the matter?" Jean-Pierre whispered.

"That's the shadow of some unfortunate person," she
murmured as she pressed closer to him. "For some
wrong he did, his shadow has become an owl and must
live in the night, deprived of the sun and its blessings."

A wolf howled.

"Ah, little brother," she chanted softly. "Why so sad?
It sounds as if you have lost something precious. Will
you ever find it again?"

She pondered the smoke that ringed the great yellow moon. The river resounded all around them. The rapids roared, their cascades frozen in the moonlight. Nothing moved. Yet everything had a sound and a scent—the wolf, the rocks, the stars.

Leaf patterns fell upon them, speckling their bodies with shadow.

He turned slowly, and the image of the branches wove an ornamental net across his thighs. His long black hair spread across Amana's breast like a single spray of water.

"Will you untie your braids and let down your hair for me, Amana?" he whispered.

She smiled slowly as she unfastened the thongs from her braids, and she sighed as her long heavy hair fell about her shoulders.

"And will you take off your belt and your moccasins for me?"

She hesitated, touching the snakeskin belt that prevented pregnancy. Then she shook her head apologetically.

"Not the belt. The belt is from my grandmothers— I must keep the belt," she murmured, slipping out of her moccasins and pressing her bare toes into the deep grass.

"Why must you keep it, Amana? It is only a snakeskin sash. I will give you an eagle feather for it," he said, smiling.

"It is something I must keep for myself," she said softly, stroking his hair. "We must all keep something of ourselves, Jean-Pierre Bonneville. That is what I have learned from the bad days. We must have ourselves and we must also have a people to whom we belong . . . a people with a belief in us . . . a people who know that we exist." And then Amana paused and a sad look came over her dark face. "It is terrible, Jean-Pierre Bonneville, not to have a people. It is terrible to be abandoned, to be cast out and forgotten. And so, do you see, I must keep something from those faraway summers, or nothing will remain of them."

The wolf howled and Amana sighed. She began to speak again, but Jean-Pierre put his mouth to her lips gently. Slowly, they retreated into each other, limb upon limb. He was as hard and as sleek as a colt. He smelled like berries and horses.

"Do you like being here with me?"

"Yes."

"And do you want to live with me, Amana?"

"Yes, I want to live with you."

And then they rolled slowly into the wet grass, and the night was perfectly white in the moonlight.

They came together hesitantly, filling the space between them softly, slowly, until the moon disappeared behind their eyes and the grass began to sing its long green song. Even the spider had vanished, leaving its luminous silver trellis in the air.

And the night stretched out in the moonlight, arching its back where the mountains rose and sending up mist where the river tumbled moment by moment into the grassy valley.

* * *

In the days that followed, they stayed together at the trading post, hanging large buffalo skins in the windows so Hugh Monroe, Jean-Pierre's partner, could not look in on them when they were making love. Day and night they could hear him grunting drunkenly or pacing back and forth, his solid boots beating a persistent rhythm on the floorboards.

Amana disliked Hugh Monroe, but gradually she came to feel sorry for him. He was not a happy man. He seemed like an animal separated from his own kind, wheeling, darting, going nowhere, waiting for a call that was never sounded, for a signal that was never given. And when he was drunk, his sorrow turned to bitterness and self-contempt. He thrived on caustic remarks and sarcasm. Gradually Amana recognized that he was utterly impotent, a pathetic man who lacked even the capacity to be a brute.

When Jean-Pierre was at home, Amana and Hugh Monroe rarely spoke to one another, but when Jean-Pierre went hunting, suddenly Monroe would lurch into conversation as if he had wrenched a gag from his mouth. He spoke to Amana insistently, even if she did not listen. He spoke nonsense, describing the room in which they were seated, pacing to and fro and conversing endlessly in a loud voice. He would not stop speaking. He talked as if his life depended upon it, as if silence would kill him.

If Amana went outside, he would follow her. And when she closed a door behind her, he stood on the other side, still talking.

As the weeks passed, Amana became so accustomed to his sad, persistent voice that she missed it when Jean-Pierre returned. Then, quite suddenly, Hugh Monroe would cease to speak. He shuffled about his work in abject silence, and the house creaked gently in every gust of wind, sighing from its rafters.

Amana sometimes suspected that Hugh Monroe's silence when Jean-Pierre was at home was some kind of punishment, some kind of retribution for her intrusion into their lives.

There were many things Amana hoped to learn about Jean-Pierre: about his family and his life before she had met him. But he never talked about himself, and Amana could not bring herself to ask Hugh Monroe the very questions she suspected he longed to answer.

"I could tell you some stories about your Monsieur Bonneville," Hugh Monroe would sputter when Jean-Pierre went off and they were alone again.

But Amana turned away and would not listen.

"I have known him a long time—nine years maybe. I've known him since he first came west from Montreal."

"Be quiet," Amana muttered. "I am not interested in your stories."

"He wasn't more than maybe twenty-one when he came west. The Indians called him *Mah-kwo-i-wo-ahts* . . . Rising Wolf. They liked him from the first time they set eyes on him at the trading post. And so the elders gave him a name. But it didn't mean a thing to Jean-Pierre Bonneville. He already had a very good name of his own. What did he need with an Indian name? So he just thanked the elders and went about his business. Yeah," Hugh Monroe babbled. "I could sure tell you something about your Monsieur Bonneville."

"Stop it!" Amana cried out in despair. Hugh Monroe drew back in surprise. And then, before he could start talking once again, she hurried from the house and leaped bareback upon her pony and galloped far out into the open plain.

She rode toward Amalia's cabin for the first time since she had left with Jean-Pierre almost half a year ago. She missed her friend. She missed having a friend . . . the company of another woman . . . the secrets, the jokes, the freedom from the bravado of men.

As Amana neared the house, she pulled up abruptly, uncertain if Amalia would welcome her. "This is foolish," she murmured, and she galloped forward.

The cabin was dark and silent. The front door stood ajar, and there was Amalia's rusty steamer trunk half buried in the dead grass near the doorway.

Amana slipped silently from her pony and made her way through the deep thicket. She listened for some sign of Amalia. But the only sound from the house was the wind whistling through its open windows and doors.

"Amalia!" she exclaimed in dread.

There was no reply . . . just the whining of the wind.

Slowly Amana approached the trunk and, digging aside the grass, fumbled at the latch until it opened. She lifted the lid and her eyes filled with tears. Amalia had put all Amana's belongings into the trunk and left it abandoned outside.

The house was deserted. And Amalia had gone away without saying good-bye.

*   *   *

Nothing that remained in the world was familiar to Amana. The land was no longer the place she had known as a girl. Everything was changing, and she could not find the center. When Jean-Pierre went away, she was afraid. She was afraid of the doors, the chairs, the dust upon the windowsills, the cups, the plates, the little fire imprisoned in a stove of iron.

She was a stranger in her own house. Instead of buckskins she wore a cotton dress because she thought it would please Jean-Pierre. She sat on chairs. And she spoke a language that was not her own. The words of her youth slipped away from her day by day, like blood flowing from her heart. Without these words she felt weak and defenseless, like something new and as yet unformed. And this sense of not being herself frightened her more than anything else, because she dreaded what she was becoming.

She had many dreams, but she awakened without any memory of her visions. They slipped away and left her dreamless. She dreaded the emptiness of her sleep.

Then, as the sun was fading from the sky, Jean-Pierre would return to the cabin with fresh elk meat and a large basket of berries. Hugh Monroe would stop in the middle of a sentence when the door opened and Jean-Pierre stepped into the trading post.

"What have you two been doing all day?" Jean-Pierre would ask.

Amana would frown and shake her head in confusion. Then she would hug him and press herself eagerly against him. And he would smile his bright, innocent smile.

But no sooner had he come home from a long absence than he was ready to leave again. The next morning he would rise at dawn and build a fire and make breakfast before going hunting. He liked to be off by himself.

When Jean-Pierre left, the quiet vanished. Instantly Hugh Monroe began talking again. There were no pauses between his sentences. He seemed to want to bury Amana in words.

And so the summer passed. The moon lingered in the daytime sky like a faded sun. The long pods of milkweed twisted lazily in the gigantic heat of the day and then burst into cloudy seeds that thickened the wind and turned the air white. Then one day, in the solitude of the cool storeroom, Amana loosened the snake belt that had been given to her by her grandmothers. She took the belt from around her waist and hid it under the tool bin.

*   *   *

Now it was time to move the trading post to a new location for the winter months. Hugh Monroe's bull train pulled in. He had hired three good axemen to help build the new post and a couple of cabins. At last Jean-Pierre and Amana would have a cabin to themselves!

"Damn Indians never stay in one place!" Hugh Monroe muttered resentfully. "Got to drag ourselves after them like a bunch of tinkers! Lord, what I'd give for a good job in the mines. What I'd give for a nice fat woman on my knee every night—without all this chasing after Indians!"

Before daybreak they were ready to leave their summer home and search for winter grounds where the tribes would be hunting and tanning their pelts for trade.

They set out for a location on Back Fat Creek, not far from the foot of the Rockies, and less than a hundred miles from Fort Benton. It seemed to Monroe and Jean-Pierre an ideal camp for the winter.

Jean-Pierre took charge of one wagon and Amana drove the other. Hugh Monroe, full of liquor, loped along on his mare, leaning far back in the saddle and steadily watching Amana through glazed eyes.

"Now take your Jean-Pierre Bonneville. . . ." His voice was slurred as he bobbed along, tilting to and fro in the saddle. "He never seen an Indian till he came out here. He was so damn green when he came stumbling here from Montreal—well, just take a look at him now, he still looks like he pees in his britches! He's just green by nature. Green clear through and never will grow up."

Amana prodded the horses, hoping to overtake Jean-Pierre, but the lead wagon was far ahead.

"Well, Jean-Pierre left Montreal for the wild west! His mother gave him a pair of dueling pistols and a prayer book." This combination of objects seemed so ridiculous to Hugh Monroe that he howled with laughter, pausing just long enough to take a swig from his jug. "Can you beat that—dueling pistols . . . my God . . . what did they think he was going to be doing out here anyway? There's nobody out here within two thousand miles willing to defend his honor. . . . So anyway, they gave him these fool pistols and a prayer book, and then the family priest gave him a rosary and told him to say a whole lot a prayers—and they sent him way the hell out here to find his fortune!" Hugh Monroe shook with laughter.

"Aih," Amana sighed impatiently, "for you everything is funny. I do not understand. I only understand that you laugh far too much for someone who is happy. I think maybe, Hugh Monroe, that you cannot decide if you love or hate Jean-Pierre Bonneville. And I think it makes you a little crazy."

Monroe peered at Amana. It seemed as if he might suddenly cry out in pain, so terrible was the expression in his eyes. Then he staggered off his horse into the snow and stood with his head thrown back, howling.

Amana watched him. For a long time Hugh Monroe stood knee deep in the drifts and cursed the sky.

"You are drunk," Amana said finally. "One day, if

you are not careful, I will tell Jean-Pierre the crazy things you tell me about him!" Then she lashed the horses and moved far ahead.

*   *   *

The winter post was established. Jean-Pierre and Hugh Monroe awaited the arrival of the various bands of Indians who would be setting up their own winter encampments in the region. The shelves were stocked with flour, sugar, tea, beads, and whiskey. The empty storeroom was ready for the arrival of the buffalo robes and skins the Indians would barter for supplies.

When Amana complained to Jean-Pierre about Hugh Monroe, he only embraced her and did not listen to what she was trying to tell him. He laughed boyishly as he pressed himself against Amana and gazed at her without really seeing her.

Amana cried out, pushing Jean-Pierre away. "Please! Listen to me, Jean-Pierre! Will you please *listen*!"

"You are upset," he whispered, trying to kiss her. "Everything will be all right. You must trust me."

"But you are not listening to me," she began urgently. Then abruptly she fell silent as she discovered a terrible vacancy in Jean-Pierre's eyes. Had it always been there? She stepped back with a dazed gesture and studied him.

"You must trust me," he repeated.

Amana did not speak. She tried to see in him the young man she loved so desperately.

"Trust me," he whispered.

"Yes . . . yes," she said listlessly, as a sense of confusion and loss filled her. And then she turned away, wandering aimlessly into their bedroom.

The room Amana and Jean-Pierre shared had a large, simple mud fireplace. Amana kept it burning brightly so the cabin would be warm and comfortable. There were two wooden chairs and there was also a very large bed. It was Amana's first bed. And she didn't like it.

The bed was very soft and it was wide, but Amana thought she might fall out of it. It was strange and unnatural sleeping so far from the earth. She refused to make love in the bed. And when Jean-Pierre was away at Fort Benton, she curled up on the floor near the fireplace, where she could smell the strong stench of smoke and timber.

Their room also contained a handsome little bureau that Jean-Pierre had ordered from Montreal. Amana had never seen anything so beautifully made. The wood was perfect. And the drawers could be opened and closed, and each one of them had a little silver handle. Someone had taken great care in making that fine piece of furniture. Amana dusted and polished it, arranging and rearranging its contents. In the bottom drawer she kept her fox medicine bundle.

Jean-Pierre had even ordered draperies for the two windows. He showed Amana how to tie them back with blue ribbons. He did everything possible to make their room look like a French home. The only thing he forgot to order was a dining table. And since Amana knew that white men did not like to eat on the ground, she spent one day making a table from a large packing case. She covered it with a bright-colored blanket.

"Very pretty, very pretty," Hugh Monroe muttered with a sour expression. "Very pretty indeed. We are becoming a regular little housewife, aren't we?"

"Be quiet," Amana said flatly. "I am not interested in your opinions."

"Jean-Pierre loves all of this. To him this whole place, this whole country, is some sort of marvelous game. In Montreal he could do anything. He could be absolutely anything . . . he could come and go as he liked . . . free and rich and respectable. Tip his hat to all those good-looking ladies and count the money in his father's bank. But instead he gets sent out here to this godforsaken wilderness to make his own fortune! And instead, he takes up with an Indian."

Amana winced. She turned away and continued to arrange the blanket on the makeshift table.

"I'm sorry," Hugh Monroe murmured in a strange, gentle voice she had never heard before. "I don't mean any harm. But you should watch out for yourself. You don't understand men like us. I start wondering what you're going to do when you find out what a rotten bunch of liars we are!"

He put his jug on the new table and walked out of the room.

*   *   *

The post was barely completed when the tribes began to arrive. Three thousand Indians pitched their lodges along a wide valley below the location of the trading post. Jean-Pierre passed the greater part of his time down in the camps with a young Indian named Weasel Tail. They were old friends. Together they gambled with the wheel and arrows, and with the bone concealed in the players' hands. Jean-Pierre had even mastered the complicated gambling song that was sung while the hand game was being played. He was chanting merrily to himself as he rode back to the post with a present for Amana. She watched him as he approached, more perplexed than ever by this stranger who was her lover. He kissed her and handed her the gift.

"It's beautiful," she exclaimed. He spread the buffalo-skin couch on the floor and set up backrests at each end.

"Now," he said gently, "perhaps you will sleep better."

"You are not angry with me," she whispered. "You are not disappointed about the bed, are you?"

Jean-Pierre smiled broadly. "We will look at the bed and we will sleep on the floor," he said fondly.

*　　*　　*

By November a large group of Blackfeet had come down from the north, where they had been summering along the Saskatchewan. And following them by a few days were Amana's own people, the Blood. She peeked out from the trading post door, uncertain if her tribe would laugh at her long dress.

She was reluctant to go outside, but when she heard the voices of the people and when she saw the familiar designs of their lodges, she began to sing with happiness. Many of the words that had been lost leaped back into her mind. She felt like an Indian again! She rushed out the door and leaped onto her horse and raced into the valley, searching faces for someone she knew.

There were new babies, born during the big summer hunt. And there were new wives, stolen during raids against the Crow or courted during the hunt when families from different bands brought their handsome daughters to the encampments.

"My brother," she called to a young hunter, "do you know a woman of the Gros Ventres . . . a woman with a bad face and a distraught mind who is called Yellow Bird Woman?"

"No," he said politely, smiling at Amana. "I do not know such a woman, but if I should see her I will tell her that you have asked for her. My name is Eagle Son and I will tell her."

"My name is Amana . . . and I thank you, brother," she murmured, delighted by the sound of her own language.

Soon the elders approached and greeted her. Amana sighed as each of her tribal leaders nodded his welcome. Their faces were filled with the grief and hardship of many bad winters, and those who had survived were so haggard and emaciated that she could not easily recognize them.

"Come, Amana," they said solemnly. "There are few of us left from the days when we were free. Come and sit with us, for you know these white men, and we have many grave questions about them."

"Come, Amana. Sit with us. We are no longer arrogant men who disdain the council of women. All our pride has vanished with the buffalo."

As Amana entered the lodge, tears filled her eyes, for she was surrounded by a faint scent of old men; and this fragrance brought back memories of Far Away Son, the generous old man who had once been her husband; who had protected and defended her; who had stood up for her among these very same elders when they had criticized her for wanting to live the life of a hunter and warrior.

When they had feasted and smoked, the men sat silently. Amana waited patiently for them to speak. They looked at her for a long time. Then Red Crow said, "How is it with these *na-pe-koo-wan* . . . these white people?"

When Amana did not respond, he continued, "You live among them now. You understand what they say. How is it with them, Amana?"

"They are strange people. I will admit to you that I find them unlike any I have known. But they are friends of the Blood."

Her answer did not seem to satisfy the tribal leaders. Their stern expressions when they spoke of white men surprised and worried Amana. When she had lived among her people, they had accepted the European strangers as the people of another tribe. It was acceptable for an Indian to take a wife or a husband from among them. But now their question betrayed a terrible breach that separated Indians from whites. And from the faces of the elders Amana realized that for them she lived in that breach and was both admired and distrusted.

For a long time the men were silent. Then Red Crow said, "You understand many things. You were once given a great vision. You can see without your eyes. What is it that you see, Amana?"

She did not know what to say to these elders whose ancient wisdom had kept her people alive. She could not tell them that her vision had deserted her and that she feared it would never return. She could not admit to these holy men her knowledge that the legend days were over; that an alien civilization had come, and that the animals that gave power to Indians were vanishing from the prairie because of the white men. Amana was lost in the terrible silence that existed between her tribe and white people.

Red Crow asked, "What is it these white men want, Amana?"

"I do not know."

"Why have they come here to our land?"

Amana said gravely, "They were looking for something precious—they were seeking something impossible. And then they got lost."

"What is it that they were seeking?"

"I do not know."

Red Crow nodded slowly and was thoughtful for a

long time. Then he nodded once again. "We have no wish to fight these white men. Many summers ago the Sioux sent us tobacco and greeted us. Though they have long been our enemies, they greeted us and asked us to come with them to destroy all these white men. But we did not wish to kill white men. We wished to kill Sioux."

The old men laughed quietly and touched the ground with their palms.

"We can live with these white men," Red Crow continued. "They are not our enemies. We can live with them if they will leave us in peace and make their wars with the Sioux. But the white soldiers do not know that some of us are Blackfeet and some of us are Sioux. They think we are all children of the same father. They blame us for what the Sioux have done."

"*Aih*," the elders murmured.

Then Red Crow continued: "In that great battle at the Little Bighorn many soldiers were killed. The white men are still angry at us though we did not fight. Now they only want to kill Indians."

"Will there be fighting?" Amana asked with dismay. "Will the soldiers come here?"

"We do not know," Red Crow said solemnly. "We hoped that you could tell us. You have a vision that protects you from the white man and his anger."

"I do not know," Amana stammered, looking intently at each of the old men seated around her. "They are lost. That is all I know of them. Somehow they alone among all the creatures are lost. And they have become mad with the grief of it; and in their madness and grief they need to destroy."

*   *   *

When Amana returned to the warmth of the trading post, she immediately told Jean-Pierre about her discussion with the elders. Hugh Monroe, who overheard Amana's anxious report, grunted and mumbled, "Kill every last one of these damn Indians, and then maybe we can all go back to Montreal!"

Jean-Pierre half listened to Amana when she tried to explain the dangerous situation. Then he told her not to worry about politics and soldiers.

"That's for men to worry about," he said.

"No . . . no, Jean-Pierre, you must listen to me," she entreated.

"All the wars are over, Amana," he said with a grin that was meant to be reassuring. Then he went out into the lashing snow.

"No . . . no," Amana shouted desperately over the wind, as she hurried out after him, trembling from the cold. "You must understand, Jean-Pierre! This is serious . . . this is terribly serious! We want to live in peace. We have not killed any soldiers. But these other white men, they do not know the difference between one tribe and another. They want to kill us because of what another tribe has done!"

"You will catch cold," Jean-Pierre said. "You will die of pneumonia long before you die from the bullet of a soldier." He laughed. "Go back to the cabin."

"What is the matter with you?" Amana exclaimed. "You must listen to what I am saying, Jean-Pierre. You must stop treating me like a child. You must try to understand we are in danger! Why won't you listen to me? My people are in danger, and you and I . . . all of us are in terrible danger! You must tell the elders that you understand and that you will help them against the soldiers. You must tell them you will explain that the Blackfeet are not their enemies and that we killed no one! Otherwise they will not accept you as a friend. They will look upon you as an enemy, Jean-Pierre! So you must tell them or we will die!"

Jean-Pierre pressed Amana back through the cabin door and closed it between them, saying, "All the wars are over, *ma chère.* There is no danger."

Then he disappeared into a cloud of whirling snow.

*   *   *

The lakes and streams soon froze. Within a few days there were several snowfalls, which the strong northwest winds gathered up and tossed into the coulees and onto the steep jagged slopes of the foothills. There were no buffalo. Most of the trading with the Indian hunters was done in elk, deer, and antelope pelts.

One day early in January news of a terrible massacre came up the valley. The story was passed along from tribe to tribe across the plains, and everyone who heard it wept.

"We are not friends of the Sioux," Red Crow said

at council, "but we cannot turn away when children are murdered. Big Foot is not our friend, but still we weep for all his wives and children slaughtered by the soldiers."

The old men groaned and slowly moved their eagle-feather fans in the air.

"The soldiers cried out, saying that all those who were not dead should come out of hiding and they would be safe. Little boys who were not wounded slowly crept into the clearing along with women large with child. But as soon as they came into sight, the soldiers butchered them with long knives. This is the story that has come to us from the place that is called Wounded Knee," Red Crow said softly.

The old men groaned.

Amana leaned forward in pain, and she wept bitterly for the people who had died in the snow.

"How could men do such a thing?" she murmured helplessly, while the elders gazed at her. "What kind of creature are these white men?" she shouted.

"And Hugh Monroe and Jean-Pierre Bonneville . . . these two white men who you call friends . . . what kind of creature are they?" Red Crow asked in a low, dreadful voice.

Amana's grief turned to fear.

"Are they the same men who murdered the Sioux at Wounded Knee?" Red Crow asked in a whisper.

"No! . . . no—you must not say such a thing!" she exclaimed. "Please listen to what I am saying. They had nothing to do with the massacre, any more than we had anything to do with the murders at the Little Bighorn!"

The elders glanced at one another and waited for her to continue.

But Amana was silent. She wanted to help her people. She wanted to save them from the atrocity that had occurred at Wounded Knee. But she also feared what might happen to Jean-Pierre.

"In the days ahead," Red Crow said in a grave voice, "there may be soldiers and fighting. We people of the north want peace. We do not want to fight these white men. But we will not allow our women and children and our old men to be slaughtered. We will not look away if our young men are disarmed and then murdered."

"Hugh Monroe and Jean-Pierre Bonneville have lived among us for many seasons," Amana whispered.

"Yes," Red Crow said.

"They love us and they are fair to us when we go to the trading post," Amana argued. "We cannot blame them for what happened far away. We can't blame them," she insisted.

"*Aih,*" Red Crow intoned dolefully. "Then who are we to blame?"

Amana stood up and faced the old men calmly. "How can we blame Hugh Monroe and Jean-Pierre Bonneville, who are Canadians, for the actions of the American soldiers who did this terrible thing?" she said. "They are not Americans. They do not know the faces of the soldiers who murdered the Sioux. So how can we blame them?"

Red Crow sat down and Amana quickly followed his example. He looked slowly into the faces of the elders seated all around him, and then he said, "We will love those who love us. We have never turned away from a friend. But Amana, you alone can see into the hearts of these two white men. You are strong and you have much courage. And so we must ask you to look into the hearts of these men and tell all of us that they are friends of the people. You must tell us that you trust them and that we can trust them. If they are to live among us while we are surrounded by soldiers who wish to kill us, we must know that they truly love us as much as they love you. These are the things we must hear from you if Hugh Monroe and Jean-Pierre Bonneville are to remain our friends."

Amana nodded slowly. *"Aih,"* she sighed with relief, "these things I can tell you easily. Jean-Pierre Bonneville has a love for Indian people. Though he came from far away and had never seen people like us, he gave us his friendship and he learned our language and our ways. And the elders gave him a name of honor. You can trust him with your lives as I have trusted him with mine. This I swear."

"This we too believe," Red Crow said. "But what of this man called Hugh Monroe?"

Amana frowned. Then she said, "He is strange, but

even Hugh Monroe would do nothing to harm us. He is a loyal friend of the people."

"Let us hope this is true," Red Crow murmured. "And so we will say no more of this. We will ask Sun for a good winter. We will pray that the Cold-Maker will not be angry. And we will ask that the buffalo return to our hunting grounds so our children do not starve in the cold days. As for the white man, we will leave him in peace and hope that he will leave us in peace."

*   *   *

This was the last winter of peace for the Blood. In the spring a large flotilla of steamboats was tied up at the Fort Benton levee. Among the boats were two of exceptional size and capacity, which could come upriver only once in a season—when the Missouri was overflowing from the deluge of melting snow in the mountains. It was to be their last voyage. The railroad was coming. It had already crossed into Dakota and was slowly creeping across the vast Montana plain.

When the roaring train burst into the grasslands, Amana rode out from the trading post and sat silently on a butte and watched the monstrous machine belch and huff across the land, leaving a black smudge in the perfect sky. The trains came one after another, filled with white faces, filled with people in strange clothes and hats and shoes. And for the first time these newcomers were not only men, but women and children as well.

The newcomers settled in the valleys. At first there were just a few of them, but during the spring and summer more and more families arrived. Soon they were taking over all the watering places of Red Crow's people. They began to open stores in the little towns that sprang out of the land, cutting off the ancient trails where Indians had traveled since time began. The air was dark with ash. The spirits abandoned the land and left only the brown debris of a leafless plain.

"The end of the world has come," Amana murmured as she rode through the wasteland. "The world is dying, and soon my people will also be gone."

By the trail a young woman sat weeping, and Amana dismounted and tried to comfort her.

"Are you hungry, my sister? Do you have no food? Do you have no home?"

"I have nothing," the woman wept.

"Have you no husband or family?"

"My husband is a white man," she groaned. "He was very good to me, and so I came away from my people to be with him. And then he went away and he never returned."

Amana stroked the woman's head and offered her water and food. But the woman would not eat or drink. She sobbed in misery and would not be consoled.

"Perhaps your husband was injured. Perhaps he has sent someone with a message."

"No," the woman whispered. "There is no message. There is nothing. He has abandoned me and taken up with someone else," she cried desperately.

"No . . . no . . ." Amana assured her. "He has been

delayed. He will return to you. You must go home and wait for him."

The wretched woman gazed up at Amana and an expression of fury filled her face. "He sold our home to a white man," she muttered. "He took everything and he went away with a white woman! They came to the house where I was waiting for him. And they threw me into the dirt and they laughed at me. I begged my people to help me. But they turned me out and called me a fool and said that this white man—this white coward had tricked me out of my love and my life. And when he was done with me, he left me with nothing."

Amana shuddered and embraced the woman and wept with her.

"Come . . . come, my sister; you will be my friend. You will come to the trading post and we will look after you," Amana murmured as she stroked the woman and tried to comfort her.

"No! No!" the woman cried. "Leave me! I am dead! I want nothing of the world! Turn away and leave me now, for your kindness will break my heart."

"You must not give up!" Amana pleaded. "You are young and you have much to live for!"

"I have nothing! I trusted this white man. I defied my people. I gave up my family and I gave up myself. I believed in him. I trusted him. But I was a fool. I thought I was safe from my enemies. I thought love would keep me safe. But I was wrong!"

Again Amana shuddered. She withdrew from the

woman in dread, rubbing her hands together as if attempting to remove an ill omen, a strange contamination of despair.

"Oh, leave me," the woman moaned. "Turn away and leave me now."

Slowly Amana backed away. A glistening red shadow hung motionlessly over the crouching figure by the trail.

Amana leaped onto her pony and the wind flew past her like fire, throwing up a crimson flurry of blinding sparks. When the dust cleared and Amana looked back, the woman had vanished, but the glistening red shadow remained, spreading over the desolate landscape.

*   *   *

Jean-Pierre Bonneville listened but he did not seem to hear. In their room, at night when he blew out the light, he whispered to her about love, but he did not listen.

"I am afraid," she would murmur in the dark. "I watch Red Crow and I want to weep. He stands tall and he walks straight, but behind his body is a sad old man. I watch him and I am afraid. He speaks of the greatness of the grandfathers, but he is surrounded by strangers. More and more each day Red Crow is surrounded by people who look at him as if he were already dead, as if he did not belong to this land, as if he were worn out and useless. I cannot bear it, Jean-Pierre. It breaks my heart to see it."

But Jean-Pierre did not hear what she was saying. He took her hands and pressed them. He murmured about love and he pressed himself against her. He did not listen to what she said, and he did not notice her tears on his lips when he kissed her.

And gradually Amana withdrew from his mouth and his hands. Slowly, as the light went out in his eyes, she pulled away when he reached for her. She could not sleep beside him anymore. She got up and crept toward the little bureau, listening to the snoring of Jean-Pierre; and she opened the bottom drawer where she kept her medicine bundle. She crouched before it, trying to bring a song into her mouth. She gazed at it, hoping it might still recognize her, though she had gone so far away from it that she could barely recall the good days when she had been a warrior and a hunter at the side of Far Away Son . . . when she had been part of the wide circle that held the world together and made the stars sing their glory.

There was no one left for Amana.

"Why don't you find your friend Amalia and get the hell out of here?" Hugh Monroe would mutter when she hurried through the storeroom hoping that he would not say anything to her.

"Be quiet! Be quiet and leave me alone!" she shouted.

"Well-well-you-are-not-what-I-thought-even-you-figure-it-out-may-god-help-you . . ." he mumbled.

Amana ran into her room and slammed the door. *"Aih!"* she groaned under her breath, shaking her head. *"Aih,"* she moaned, sitting on the floor and pressing her hands to her belly, feeling the steady throb deep inside her. "What am I to do now?" she sighed. "What will become of me?"

*   *   *

The white women were beautiful. Amana could not deny it. In every camp there were now many such women who had come in the train from the east. They walked strangely and they had peculiar faces hidden under their bonnets. Yet the men liked to look at them. Pale, fragile little things . . . blank-looking creatures, as helpless as infants. Yet the men liked them. And the men living with Indian women—the *squawmen*, as they were contemptuously called by the newcomers—were treated with such indignity by the white ladies that many of them had abandoned their wives or taken them and their brown children to the reserves in Canada, where life was easier.

It was the wives of the newcomers who were most bitter about squawmen. They forbade their children to play with half-breeds, and they shunned Indian wives and called them terrible names and would not be seen in their company.

There was one white man named Louis Perkins who lived with Red Crow's daughter, Calf Woman. It was a union of great honor in earlier days. But now everything was changed. Louis Perkins wanted to be sheriff of the county where the white people had built a little town of cabins and stores. He was the only candidate of his party not to be elected. The white women badgered their husbands and brothers and protested so strongly against the election of a squawman that they succeeded in defeating him.

He was very bitter, and when he came to the trading post, he complained to Amana.

"Montana hasn't been a decent place for people to live ever since those people from the east started coming out here with their crazy ideas."

"That's what some folks call progress," Hugh Monroe said.

"Ah, be quiet!" Louis Perkins exclaimed. "I'm sick to death of your smart remarks, Monroe! If you're so damn fed up with life, why don't you pack it in!"

"Come on, Louis, don't be so hard on Hugh. After all, he managed to stay sober through half the morning," Jean-Pierre said, smiling.

"Oh, the hell with both of you," Louis Perkins muttered. "I don't know what you're so smug about. Seems to me that these shopkeepers from the east are making a terrible mess out of your business too. They know how to run things. For one thing, they don't cheat people. They give their customers the right change, 'cause you can't go around tricking white folks the way you guys have been tricking Indians all these years. You can't charge white people a dollar for a lamp wick, I can tell you that much! And they don't peddle a whole lot of bad whiskey neither. So I don't know why you two are so damn pleased with the mess we're in. Seems to me that these fancy people from the city don't like either of you any better than the Indians do!"

Amana grasped the angry man's hands and tried to silence him. She looked anxiously into his face.

"I'm sorry, Amana," he murmured, "but it's no good here anymore. We can't live with these people. You can't raise a family in a place where your kids get beat up just for being half-breeds. Nobody can live here anymore."

Jean-Pierre took Amana by the shoulders and gently embraced her.

Louis Perkins gazed at the two of them. He started to turn away, but then, with an expression of grief, he whispered, "Amana—all your people are going away. No one will be left. What's to become of you now?"

She could not answer him.

"You're welcome to come with us, Amana," he said softly, while Jean-Pierre held Amana in a strong embrace.

"No . . . no," Amana gasped, shaking her head in confusion.

"It's our last chance to get away, Amana. There's nothing left for us here. There's no place for any of us anymore. It's a choice of leaving and being an Indian or staying here with these people and giving up everything you have ever been."

"No . . . no," she whimpered, his words filling her with dread.

"I'm sorry," Louis Perkins said softly, and he left her standing there, trembling.

*   *   *

One by one, these men who had married Indian women moved to the reservations. And there they settled down in the desolate bits of land set aside for them, glad to be back in a familiar world.

Amana watched her friends pack their belongings and load their wagons. And as she saw the world divide itself into two irreconcilable parts, she recalled the times when Jean-Pierre went hunting and she could feel the sick, deep wound that was made when an animal is cut away from its own kind. All these thoughts filled her mind as she watched her friends depart.

Amana had to talk with Jean-Pierre. She knew she had to shout at him, to summon her courage and raise her voice and make him understand what was happening around them. But she was afraid of what would happen if she did. Amana knew that Jean-Pierre would never leave the trading post and go to a reservation, and she knew that she would lose him if she made him see what had become of their love.

She loathed herself now because she could not speak, because she had become frightened of being alone, of being hungry and cold. She hated herself because somehow she still needed Jean-Pierre. And she hated herself because this mindless boy was the father of her unborn child. And so she pressed her hands to her belly, where she could feel her pulse throbbing, and remained silent.

Toward the end of May the trading post had to be abandoned. There was no business. The Indians were gone and the white people would not come to the post.

They preferred their own shops. One morning Hugh Monroe announced that he was leaving.

Most of the Blood and Blackfeet had moved north to summer on the Belly and Saskatchewan rivers, and the Piegans had trailed over to the Milk River and the Sweetgrass Hills. Amana asked Jean-Pierre where they would go for the summer, but he only shrugged. "That's what I've been trying to figure out," he said.

Hugh Monroe laughed as he continued packing his belongings. "Well," he said, "one thing in Jean-Pierre's favor—if everything else fails, he's got him a good Indian woman who knows how to shoot rabbits."

"Stop it!" Amana exclaimed furiously. She waited for Jean-Pierre to say something in her defense, but he simply smiled as he helped Monroe load his big trunk onto the wagon.

"You know," Hugh Monroe said, "your Monsieur Bonneville is still green. He thinks I'm a terrible rascal for cheating them poor Indian friends of his. But he never says a word to me about it. He almost did complain one day, when he found out that I had a cup with two bottoms so it holds only a little more than half as much as a real cup. And, my goodness, I think he very nearly wet his pants when he found out that I watered down the whiskey!" Hugh Monroe laughed as he slapped Jean-Pierre on the back. Then both men roared with laughter. It seemed to Amana that Jean-Pierre didn't even know what he was laughing about; he just laughed like a child, sheepishly following the example of Hugh Monroe without realizing that he was being humiliated.

"Oh, yes," Hugh Monroe exclaimed through gales of laughter, "your Monsieur Bonneville learned to live with it. He learned how to make a profit faster than you can shoot a rabbit. And he made a lot of money— all kinds of money for his wife and kids back in Montreal!"

Amana cried out and then stifled the sound with her hand. She stood up as if she had been shot. Then she whirled around and stumbled against the wall.

Surely it was a joke. That was so typical of Hugh Monroe . . . to bait her like that!

"Oooops," Hugh Monroe giggled. "Sorry, old friend, that just slipped out."

Jean-Pierre looked distressed and angry. Amana had never seen his face so clouded.

No one spoke.

Then Jean-Pierre turned away and carried the last trunk out to the wagon.

*   *   *

Amana stood at the front door, pressing her hands to her belly and staring aimlessly into the vacant landscape. Day after day she stood silently at the door. But Jean-Pierre Bonneville did not return. She continued to keep her vigil even after she knew that he would never come back to her. She stood at the door trying to disappear, trying to die, to escape from her body so the pain would not be so terrible. Of all the things she most feared, to be utterly alone was the worst. And the pain and agony of that fear wounded her in every limb, turning her stomach into a lizard and making her head crawl with a million red ants.

In dread Amana came away from the door. She lay down on her mat, and she closed her eyes, and all the people of her life stepped silently through her mind, stumbling over her tears and then disappearing into the barren land of her dream-starved sleep.

*   *   *

Two weeks later Hugh Monroe came to the trading-post door. When Amana peeked through the window and saw who was knocking, she told him to go away or she would get her rifle and shoot him. He began shouting aimlessly, the way he did when he was drunk. She opened the door and turned away from him as he strode into the room with an air of self-importance.

"Ah," he said, "this place is awful. Don't you ever sweep the floor? Jesus, the damn roof is leaking. Lady, seems to me that your house is falling down."

"You didn't come here to talk about my house, Hugh Monroe," Amana said contemptuously. "Say whatever you have come to say and then get out!"

"Well, to tell the truth," he said, "Jean-Pierre sent me to pick up one or two of his things. Nothing that you would want, just a couple of accounting books and the like."

"Well, take them and then leave," she muttered, still standing at the opposite end of the room.

He hummed a tune as he strode around, opening and closing cupboards and gathering books and papers.

"I guess you heard," Hugh Monroe was saying. "Jean-Pierre is going back to Montreal. Seems his mother is ailing."

"That's all right," Amana said so softly that Monroe could not hear her words.

"What did you say?"

"I said," she shouted, turning and glaring at him, "that that's all right with me!"

Hugh Monroe rubbed his hands together. "He's leaving and you haven't even gotten to know who he really is," he said. "The game has grown tiresome for him, Amana. Can't you see what happened?"

"He will come back. He doesn't like Montreal. He's told me so many times," she said.

"He also told you he would stay here forever. He said that too. Well, it's not fun playing cowboy when there's a whole lot of respectable folks calling you a squawman. Can't you understand that, Amana? I'm disappointed in you. All along I thought you were a really tough lady. Now it turns out you're just as dumb as all the rest."

Amana hit Monroe in the face with all her might.

He looked at her in astonishment. But then he grinned.

"Ahuh," he muttered, "then you really do realize how stupid you've been. You were a strong woman and yet you let yourself get stampeded by a man!"

Amana spat on the floor and frowned at Monroe. "I know Jean-Pierre Bonneville. I have slept with him. I have held him in my arms. I have lived with him. And I know his heart!" she said fiercely.

"Well, then, if you know him so well, Amana, tell me something: Who is he? Because I've been working with him for a long time and I can't figure it out. So tell me, who is he?"

"Please take the books and leave," Amana groaned.

"You don't want to face the facts." Hugh Monroe laughed.

"Go!"

"He's gone for good. That's what I have to tell you. He's gone for good, Amana!"

"He may be gone for good, but I swear to you that he will never forget me!"

"Ah . . . you are so foolish. If you believe that, then you don't know anything about men."

Amana cried out and rushed upon Monroe and began to strike him with all her strength, driving him from the door. A wild, long wail poured out of her.

"*Aih,*" she groaned when at last he was gone. "*Aih . . .*" Then she collapsed and lay motionless on the floor.

The wind sighed in the chimney. The night overtook the white light that fluttered in the doorway. And then a fox crept slowly from her body and fled silently into the thin dark horizon where the world comes to an end.

PART
II

There is strong shadow
Where there is much light.

GOETHE

T H R E E

It was in the winter, after Jean-Pierre had gone, that Amana's daughter was born.

A damp, chilling breeze sprang up with the sudden coming of the Cold-Maker. The snow blew against the dilapidated trading post in violent gusts. The timbers broke loose and Amana huddled in the darkness and the cold, chanting fiercely as the pain bellowed through her body. The wind was filled with the shouts of her labor.

It was during that first blizzard of winter that Jemina was born. Her mother clung to the floorboards and screamed and wept at the marvel of what was happening to her. A great mystery had filled her with new life. And Jemina was born.

It was in that same winter that a detachment of soldiers under the command of Lieutenant Crouse arrived from Fort Benton. And those few men among Amana's people who were left said nothing. They were beaten and hungry. They had grown soft under the endless siege of white men.

The soldiers took up their weapons and stationed

themselves among the lodges. The women shuddered and wept at the sight of the armed men. They feared they would be slaughtered with their children. But there was no shooting. The soldiers stood stiff and silent until Lieutenant Crouse arrived and demanded to speak to Red Crow.

"We have come to escort you and your people to the reservation," the Lieutenant said.

"On the reservation there is no game. We would have nothing to eat," the chief murmured as he stood weak with hunger and bent with humiliation.

"I am instructed to escort you to your reservation. And I am instructed to use force if necessary to carry out my orders," the soldier declared in a toneless voice.

"We must talk among ourselves," Red Crow said, gesturing to the elders who gathered wearily around the chief.

A council was held. It was not a great meeting of great men as these councils once had been. The elders were sad. They came together at the command of the soldiers; and they spoke not as leaders but as prisoners in their own land.

The elders summoned Louis Perkins, husband of the daughter of Red Crow, to join their circle, for they knew him to be a good man and they hoped that as a white man he might have some influence on their captors.

"You are one of us in your heart," Red Crow told him, "so come to our council and speak to us."

The men sat silently, looking from one to the other.

Louis Perkins shifted uncomfortably in his place, hoping that the elders would not disapprove of his silence. There was no wisdom he could offer.

"Why? Why are we treated like mischievous children?" Red Crow asked, his face ashen with grief. "Why is this done to us? By what right is it done to us? This is the land where our fathers were born. It has always been so! Who shall have the right to tell us to leave our homeland?"

No one spoke.

Then Red Crow murmured dejectedly, "Send for the soldier so we may talk with him. We have no choice. We are no longer free people."

When Lieutenant Crouse entered the council lodge, he bowed respectfully to the chief and explained that he was only an unwilling deputy who had to follow the orders of his superiors. And those orders, he said, required him to take the Indians to the agency on their reservation.

"We do not wish to go to the agency," Red Crow said in a resolute voice. "The white man who represents the Great Father at our reservation has no food, no help, no regard for us. There is no game in that region. It is a wasteland. If we go, we will starve. It is a dreadful thing to suffer for want of food. Not in our long history in this land have we been forced to live where there is nothing to eat. Pity our children, our women, our old ones. Go back to your fort and leave us here in peace."

The Lieutenant could not look at the old men seated

around him. His voice was filled with remorse when he replied that he was only a soldier required to do his duty. He urged Louis Perkins to advise the Indians to cooperate. He asked the elders not to make their removal difficult by refusing to go. Then he left the council.

Red Crow shook his head slowly. *"Aih,"* he sighed. "What can we do? Of course we could kill all these soldiers, but others would soon replace them. They would kill our women and children, even the newborn infants. My friends, we cannot fight them. Let us go to the agency and try in some way to find food and to survive. We have no choice."

That was the winter that the lodges came down, and Amana packed her belongings into a wagon and abandoned the trading post. The Indians took the trail for the north, escorted by soldiers. The horses that remained in the Indian herds were so thin and weak that many of them perished along the arduous trail. Heavily loaded wagons floundered in the drifts and had to be abandoned. The people could travel only twelve or fifteen miles each day. The old ones wept, and the children went hungry, but eventually they arrived at Fort Benton.

From Fort Benton they journeyed slowly to Fort Conrad, and then staggered onward to the desolate agency where land had been put aside for them.

It was a place of terrible poverty. Nowhere was there the track of an animal. There was nothing but wind and snow.

Amana and the other women shivered in the dreary white landscape as they pegged their few rawhides and tanned them. From the sale of these last remaining skins they purchased enough food to survive for a short time. But by the end of winter the people did not have a single skin to sell, nor anything else to barter for food.

Amana prayed while her baby slept. She opened her heart to the wind and sent a pitiful outcry into the sky. But there was nothing to eat.

"Pity me!" she cried. "I have brought this child into the world after so many summers of trouble! Always the way was difficult and filled with suffering and want. Pity me now!"

But when Amana returned to the lodge, she found her child faint and pale and groaning from hunger. Surely the little one would die.

Amana cried out and embraced her daughter. She wept until she could weep no more. Now her eyes were filled with images of her mother and father, of her sister, SoodaWa, and grandmothers Crow Woman and Weasel Woman. Everyone she had loved loomed around her as she gazed into the little fire where the kettle was filled with a terrible broth of grass and mud.

She feared she would not be able to summon the courage to live. She feared she would not have strength enough to keep her child alive. She bent forward and a shadow came over her face. She began to gasp for breath and slowly reached toward her infant.

Then suddenly she sat up. She cried out in rage and

she shook her fists, and she thrust back her head and shouted, "*Sa!* . . . No! . . . *Sa!*" again and again. "I swear to you, child," she howled. "I swear it! You will not die!"

And then she pressed her fingers into her throat and she gagged and choked until a thin froth of bile, saliva, and cud poured from her mouth. Coughing, she fed her daughter her own vomit, until the baby fell into a contented sleep.

Then Amana collapsed.

When she opened her eyes, a familiar face moved above her. She squinted, but could not recognize the features.

"Wha . . . what is this?" she stammered in confusion.

"Don't talk so many things," a voice said as warm food was gently spooned into her mouth. "Just eat and being quiet, *ma chère.*"

It was Amalia!

"You are such a foolish," Amalia muttered. "*Alors!* If this Louis Perkins friend from yours never tell me at Fort Benton how bad you are becoming here alone, I am never know my Amana has nothing . . . *rien!* Ah, *rien à manger* . . . *rien du tout! C'est terrible, ma chère* . . . *terrible!*"

"Wha . . . what is this . . . Amalia?"

"Not talking . . . not talking. Just eat, *ma chère*, so you can be living."

Amana nodded her head and smiled feebly at her friend. And then she peered anxiously toward the bed, where her child, Jemina, was asleep.

"Bien . . . très bien, ma chère. The little child she is good. You are not to worry for her. *Tout va bien mainten-ant."*

Amana sighed, and she began to sob softly as she closed her eyes. She was so weak she could not stop trembling.

"Bien . . . très bien, ma chère. Tout va bien mainten-ant," Amalia murmured as she rocked Amana's head in her lap and repeatedly brought the big spoon to her lips.

Amana wanted to talk to her friend, but she began sinking into a deep, peaceful sleep. She could not keep her eyes open and she could not speak. Soon Amalia was gone, and what remained was the face of Jean-Pierre Bonneville smiling boyishly as he hovered over her and whispered and whispered and whispered.

Amana could hear his voice, but she could not un-derstand what he was saying to her. She could not understand anything. From the darkness behind her eye-lids Jean-Pierre continued to murmur to Amana. His voice trailed like soft birds in a constant warble . . . on and on, like the chanting of wind in the trees. She tossed helplessly in her sleep, stung by the words of Jean-Pierre. Understanding nothing, but stung by the words, trying to escape them, as if they were the stones of an immense avalanche toppling down upon her.

She wanted to send Jean-Pierre Bonneville away, to order him out of her dream, but she wanted to show him their child. She wanted to show him the tiny feet and hands of his daughter. But she could not bear the avalanche of words. She could not bear the weight of the pain that pressed down upon her dreams.

Gradually the voice of Jean-Pierre Bonneville withered and withdrew, and Amana opened her eyes.

Amalia smiled and hugged her old friend. Then she put the child on the mat next to Amana and nodded with tears in her eyes. "Such a *jolie* . . . such a pretty child, *ma chère.*"

"I was afraid she might be ugly," Amana whispered, looking down at Jemina. "I was afraid she would be a deformity . . . that she would be ugly because her father was a French-Canadian. Because I was stupid and would not listen when you told me he was not a good man."

"Hush, my friend," Amalia murmured. "It is over now . . . all over. And the child is *jolie.*"

"Ah," Amana groaned when she thought of Jean-Pierre. "How I hate that Canadian! How I loved him and now how I hate him! I was afraid my hate would make my baby into a monster."

"*Oh, sacré,*" Amalia exclaimed. "*Mon Dieu*, but that is a terrible thing to say, *ma chère*! My father . . . that *bâtard* . . . he was *français* . . . and look how I am turning out so *jolie*! All the mans Fort Benton they like and say how I am *assez jolie*! And I make plenty and care nothing what they are thinking for me." She laughed loudly. "*Alors!*" Amalia whispered as she gazed at the baby. "Always I am so much loud. Poor baby wake up from me."

Amana smiled at her friend. "You are a good person

and a good friend to me," she murmured. "A better friend to me than I was to you, Amalia."

"Shhh . . . *taisez-vous, ma chère. S'il vous plaît*, all that is forgetting. Promise not such bad idea for us to talk, Amana. *Amies* . . . friends is what we are and for friends everything is always good . . . *très bien toujours . . . toujours bien!*"

Amana touched her friend's face gently and peered into her eyes, in which the bad years had left nothing but grief.

"*Ma chère,*" Amalia wept bitterly, as if she understood Amana's thoughts. "It has been a hard life for both of us. You are not to worry anymore. *Oui, ma chère?* Listen for me . . . and when you feeling good and better, we two of us are going for Fort Benton. I got pretty good business by Fort Benton. And then maybe we ask some mans for idea to help the child. *Oui, ma chère?* But now you are rest. Resting . . . resting . . . resting . . . that is what you are do, *ma chère.*"

*   *   *

"D'know how to speak English?" the man muttered as he looked at Amana disapprovingly.

"Yes . . . yes, I can speak," she stammered eagerly when Amalia gave her a sharp nudge.

"Well, maybe we can use you in the kitchen, seeing you're a friend of Amalia's," he said in a flat, nasal voice.

"Kitchen? Why kitchen?" Amalia exclaimed. "She good woman, could maybe serve customers."

"Listen, Amalia," he complained with a sour look, "you run your business and let me run mine. No way I can have an Indian waiting on customers, y'hear? No way."

"Kitchen?" Amalia asked meekly with raised brows.

"That's right . . . kitchen," the man said. "Ten dollars a week and all the food you want, 'cept none of that canned stuff from St. Louis. And no whiskey allowed and Indians don't do no talking to the customers. You savvy that, girl?"

"She savvy . . . she savvy," Amalia assured Mr. Fuller as she hurriedly bid him good-bye and pulled Amana out of his sight as quickly as possible.

"But Amalia . . . Amalia," Amana objected as her friend dragged her through the door. "I know nothing of restaurants," she insisted.

"*Mon Dieu, taisez-vous, ma chère!* Know restaurant, know nothing for restaurant . . . what difference, uh?" Amalia said sternly. "How much you need to know to wash dishes? You understand what Amalia saying for you? You work kitchen Mr. Fuller, you stay my place, you make lots money, you have good food, you have things for Jemina . . . all this, *ma chère*! Nothing to it, *ma chère*. Just listen your Amalia. So . . . now, *ma chère*, you agree, *oui* . . . you washing dishes Mr. Fuller, yes?"

"Washing dishes Mr. Fuller yes," Amana agreed with a weary smile.

"Ah, *merde!* You making fun for your Amalia! Shame for you!" she huffed as she embraced Amana. "Now we go my place and you find out sure what kind big success I am having here by Fort Benton, *ma chère.* You find out what fantastic place your Amalia have! *Chez Amalia! Alors, c'est très élégant, ma chère!* Wait for you seeing!"

Amana and Amalia stepped out into the brisk winter's morning. They made their way carefully past the men unloading provisions from wagons in front of Mr. Fuller's Fine Restaurant.

"Best place in Fort Benton for whiskey and meal," Amalia assured her friend. "Very respectable. Best place but for Chez Amalia!"

Horses lurched and splashed through the muddy street as the two women lifted their skirts and hurried across.

"*Merde!* What place is this Fort Benton!"

White curls of smoke rose from the chimneys of the squat wooden houses. Trees and grass had been stripped from the land, and the post office, drugstore, church, a few homes, and Mr. Fuller's Fine Restaurant sat starkly in the gray dust.

Tall poles leaning at odd angles were twisted with telegraph and telephone wires. Signs and placards covered every wall and roof. The side street that led to Amalia's house was piled high with so much debris from houses remodeled or torn down that it was nearly impassable. Dogs barked and trotted through the puddles, scattering from the wheels of the hurtling wagons, and then scrambling back into the gutters to devour the heaps of refuse tossed there by shopkeepers and housewives.

There were people everywhere, hurrying and talking in many different languages. The steamboat was docking, moving noisily against the gray sky as it made its laborious way to the shore. The wharf was filled with workmen, children, and animals. And people began to shout as the boat rumbled into the moorings and a steady flow of emigrants staggered to shore with their pathetic belongings and poured like rats into the muddy streets. The river had been harnessed. The animals and trees had been exiled. And nothing remained but this place of fabulous decay.

"Look for you, Amana!" Amalia exclaimed when the two women sat alone in the splendid parlor. "Look what I done here!"

Amana had never seen such a peculiar house.

"You see, *ma chère* . . . rope portieres, Turkish leather rockers, glass Bordeaux lamps, Deluxe Talking Machine for the *musique*, everything perfect, *oui?*"

Amana nodded in amazement. "Is all of this yours?"

"Yes! All belong for Amalia! I make plenty money and I order all things from Sears and Roebuck book. What you think for your Amalia now?"

"But how can you make so much money? How can one woman make so much money from the white people?"

"Oh," huffed Amalia with an elegant gesture of her hand. "Takes more than one womans. I got six. I got six girls and Fort Benton got one hundred mans! So you figure this out, yes." Then Amalia laughed boisterously. "And *that* make lots for money, *ma chère!*"

Amana shook her head in dismay. "*Aih*, Amalia, so you are still sleeping with all the men."

"Puff . . . look for me, *ma chère.* I too much old for flirting around. Those mans, they stop want Amalia long time ago. So how I live, huh? How does Amalia still live when white mans say she old? My gollies, I nearly die. But soon some young womans are now coming for Fort Benton. White girls, Indians girls, who knows what kind girls—no money, no husband, no nothing. So Amalia is thinking, if I too old for these mans, I get these girls working in my house. They stay Chez Amalia. One, two, three mans are coming. Then many mans. I buy house. Fix *très élégant! Et voilà, ma chère,* we sit nice and comfort with your little Jemina up in your room sleeping in nice bed! Everything fine. We live. We eat. We not die from hungry. And, for last of life, everything finally marvelous . . . *n'est-ce pas, ma chère?*"

Amalia gazed at her friend, and suddenly her gay mood changed. "So look for you," she whispered. "Look for you, Amana. What have they done to you? Already you old woman. Ah, these mans . . . what they do with us, *ma chère?* All years passing us and now look how we old ladies already. No husband, no lover . . . just old women all alone for ourselves. . . ."

The two friends looked fondly at one another. And Amana nodded sadly. Yes, they had changed. Amalia was growing old and Amana had aged beyond her years, and all the hardship had found its way into their faces. Amana sighed as she gazed at Amalia. Her face was painted. A heavy mask of powder covered her sagging jowls and matted the deep wrinkles under her eyes. Her black skin had faded to an ashen clay color. Her hair was thin and dyed. Her full breasts sagged against one another, and her neck hung in two large folds of flesh.

"*Oui, c'est vrai, ma chère*—these mans, they ruin us. They have no strength. They take all strength from us. All they know is what they wanting from us. That is all for them. Then we old and they say *adieu* . . . good-bye. And sometime they not even say *à bientôt*. They go and you and me, Amana, we remain."

"And are you well?" Amana whispered.

"Sure . . . sure. The body goes on. I feel good. Maybe four years now I stop to drinking. Nothing I drink—not one glass whiskey. And I got good lungs and heart. I fine, *ma chère*. But you—you have had bad times."

"We are not like the white people," Amana murmured with a weary gesture of her hand. "We are Indians. And when we sit down in one place for too long, we get old. And then we die. In our hearts we die."

"But now you live good with me, Amana. All dying day is finished. Now begins the living, *ma chère*!"

Amana nodded with a grateful smile and took Amalia's hand. The women wept silently.

"And what for that pig—that Jean-Pierre Bonneville? Why for he does nothing for his own baby? That man is pig!" Amalia huffed in anger. "Ah, these mans! These mans! All they know is what they wanting for us. That is all for them!"

"I don't think about him anymore," Amana lied. "He was a foolish boy. That's why he was nice. That's why I loved him. He never really meant to hurt me. It was just a game for him. For him it was only a little dream that he was dreaming."

"*Oui, c'est vrai, ma chère.* The mans have no strengths. They have no hearts. The only pain they feel is their own pain. They use us. That is all for them. A warm bed, a warm woman, someone looking after them like children. Not only Jean-Pierre Bonneville, but all them. Every one of these mans is play with us."

The two friends looked lovingly at one another. Pain filled the space between them, turning them into a single person; turning the pain into a single pain that they both perfectly understood.

*   *   *

And so Amana washed dishes at Mr. Fuller's restaurant. The white people gave her a dish rag and a large bar of yellow soap, and then they forgot about her.

Mr. Fuller was the cook. He shouted at the men who waited on the customers and they shouted at the bartender. And the years passed.

The men sat at the tables in their black pants and black jackets and black hats. They shouted at one another. And Amana washed dishes from six in the morning until six at night. Then she collected $1.42 and went home to Chez Amalia, where Jemina sat with the whores in the parlor, looking at the pictures in *The Ladies' Home Journal.*

"Look at this, Mother!" the child exclaimed. "Look at these fine ladies! Aren't they beautiful!"

Amana nodded, glancing at the pictures of statuesque white women in elaborate fashions.

"Aren't they marvelous!" Jemina murmured, self-consciously imitating the women of Chez Amalia.

Again Amana nodded, distressed by the child's limited vision of life. She wanted to embrace Jemina, to hold her so close that she would become part of her body again. She wanted to teach her the lessons of the grand-mothers, to give Jemina all the precious things that Weasel Woman and Crow Woman had given her. But Jemina had gotten lost in the world of Chez Amalia . . . in dreams of great cities and rich men and fancy shops. Amana could no longer touch Jemina. She could not talk to her. The child loved only finery. She wanted everything she saw in magazines. She knew nothing of the unspoiled world beyond Fort Benton: the forest that lay like an ancient book in which all the good things of the creator, Napi, were written.

"Shall we take the wagon and drive far out into the open prairie?" Amana would ask.

"Oh, Mother, no. It will ruin the new dress Amalia made for me."

Amana nodded sadly and stroked the child's hair. And when the gentlemen started knocking at the door, Amana took Jemina upstairs to their room and sat with her on the big bed and told her stories of Napi, the Old Man, who had made the world and everything in it. But Jemina wasn't interested in Napi. She wanted to go downstairs where there was music and dancing. She wanted to hear the traveling men talk about Cincinnati and St. Louis. And when the Deluxe Talking Machine began to make a strange music in the parlor downstairs, Jemina pranced around the room, doing a dance she had learned from the whores. Then Amana would sigh and gaze over her daughter's shoulder into a past she could no longer see clearly. She whispered broken phrases, faintly gasping when the precious words would not come to mind. The words were lost in the abyss into which faces, names, and events were gradually vanishing. The past was closing itself away, remote and distant from the strange life of the present. Amana nodded as she gazed at things that no longer existed. It was no wonder little Jemina didn't understand them.

And the years passed.

Jemina turned thirteen. While Amana sat in the sunshine, musing on the swift passage of the years, a man came to the door and asked to speak to her. He was from the government, he said, and required information about Amana's daughter.

"I'm sorry . . . I will call for a friend," Amana stammered nervously.

A young woman named Adella joined the guest in the parlor and sat next to Amana. Then the man said: "I am here because we have a report that your daughter has never been enrolled at the Indian school provided for the children of your people. We also have no record that she has ever attended the mission school. Do you understand what I am saying? It is my duty to inform you that all Indian children must attend one of the schools designated by the government. Do you understand this law, madam?"

Amana glanced anxiously at Adella.

"She has good learning . . ." Amana said.

"Of course she does," Adella insisted. "Jemina is getting a fine education right here at home!"

"Is that the child's name?" the man asked, ignoring the women's comments and meticulously writing in his book. "Jemina Bonneville? Is that the child's name?"

"Of course it is," Adella huffed. And then, looking at Amana, she told her, "Don't pay any attention, Amana; you have a perfect right to educate Jemina any way you like."

"Indian children," the man said flatly, "are required by law to attend a school designated by the government. Indian children are wards of the government. . . ."

"But . . . but . . ." Amana said helplessly, a look of fear coming into her face.

"This is silly!" Adella exclaimed. "Now you just get out of here this minute or I'll call for help and have you thrown out!"

The man raised his brows and looked Adella up and down. "This is no place for a child. There are good women in Fort Benton who have lodged complaints.

And it is my duty to inform you that the child will be taken away and put in school. She will not be allowed to remain in this house. Indian children must go to government schools. That is the law."

"This isn't a reservation, and Jemina's father wasn't an Indian, and you don't have any right to come in here!" Adella shouted.

The man interrupted: "I'm not going to argue with you, madam. I'll make my report, and then you'll see what happens!"

"Adella!" Amana exclaimed as the man slammed the door behind him. "I am afraid!"

*   *   *

Amana slowly packed Jemina's suitcase and embraced her daughter with tears in her eyes. The little girl was baffled by her mother's sorrow. She ran jubilantly from room to room, kissing all the whores good-bye and shouting with excitement when the carriage arrived to take her to boarding school.

"Now be good girl," Amalia beseeched incessantly as the suitcase was loaded into the carriage. "Be good girl; be very good girl," Amalia repeated. "And don't talk anybody. Nobody talking for you, *ma chère.* No talking especially for the mans!"

Amana put her hands on either side of Jemina's head, and for a moment she looked at her so intently that the child became confused. *"Puh-po-kan,"* Amana whispered.

"What—what did you say, Mother?" Jemina asked.

"Say it in English—say it so I can understand."

The coach started to move. In an instant the other women swept between the mother and daughter, waving. Amana's breast ached as she gazed past them into a place she could no longer see clearly. "Dream," she whispered. *"Puh-po-kan . . .* do not forget how to dream, little one."

Then Jemina was gone.

*   *   *

"Believing for me," Amalia assured her friend. "Far better Jemina is going for Miss Wells' Girls' School than Indian school of government, where all the children learn is how to work in other people's homes. Believing for me, Amana."

Amana did not respond. She sat silently, staring at the parlor floor, torn apart.

"Believing for me, Amana, you make good decision. Please, *ma chère*, you breaking my heart seeing you like this. Believe your Amalia . . . nothing can do with these dirty government mans. They take Jemina to Indian school and there will be nothing for you to do. But now she is far away in Canada at Miss Wells' Girls' School, and nothing they can do!"

"Aih," Amana moaned.

"It good school. Only best girl go for this school, Amana. Believing for what I tell you, *ma chère*! Adella very smart for things. She swear this boarding school very elegant home for girls, and lady who is running it very smart British named Miss Wells."

Amana exclaimed, "Why couldn't she stay here? Everything was fine when she lived here with us!"

"Now, Amana, *ma chère*, we talked about same thing how many time? How such a little girl live in Chez Amalia? With mans they coming and going and the ladies are saying terrible gossips for all times and the children run loose like little animals in street—what kind of life little Jemina have for such place like this, Amana?"

"But I wanted her to spend the summers with Louis Perkins and Red Crow. Now that she is a young woman, I wanted her to learn the words of my people . . . the tales of our days . . . the secrets of the grandmothers," Amana said with growing dismay.

"At the government school they treat her like trash. You know all of this, Amana."

Adella came into the parlor and gazed sympathetically at Amana. "Amalia is right," she whispered. "Jemina will have a new life. You don't want your daughter to turn out like us, now do you, Miss Amana? Why, of course you don't. And so you have got to try to understand that the only way she's going to make anything of herself is if she gets a good education. And Miss Wells runs a nice school. She has all her young ladies learn how to behave themselves in a real stylish English way. At the government school they learn nothing— just how to be servants, how to do laundry and wash dishes and clean other people's houses. I wish I had been sent to Miss Wells. She teaches them how to drink tea and fancy ways of cooking and dressing and putting up their hair. Take my word for it, Miss Amana. You don't want Jemina in one of those government Indian schools. Miss Wells' School is the right place to have sent her. Costs a pretty penny, but it's worth every cent!"

"Aih," Amana said slowly. "I want what is good for Jemina. I don't know anything about schools. But if you say this gives her a better life and I must send my Jemina away, then I must do it. I want her to be happy."

And so Jemina had gone away, and Amana washed dishes at Mr. Fuller's Fine Restaurant. Mr. Fuller shouted at the waiters and the waiters shouted at the bartender and the men who sat at the tables in their black pants and jackets shouted at one another. Amana washed dishes and then she went home to Chez Amalia, where she put her earnings in a bottle. Each week she went with Mr. Fuller to the post office, and he got a money order for her and mailed it to Miss Wells' Girls' School.

And time passed.

*   *   *

The rains came and after them came the suns of many months. The silence was shattered by the chatter of birds that beat the air with their wings as great wounds appeared in the forest, as trees fell, as nests of many seasons crumbled. Now the birds were silent, and the song of the axe was the only song heard in the forest.

(Amana lay on her mat and closed her eyes, trying to imagine Jemina and wondering if she was lonely during all these long months.)

Wild figs were born among the broken branches of

the pines, and after a while they made a leafy tomb over the great wounds of the forest. Then came the rains that pulled away the earth, cutting deep where the bones of generations of animals were hidden. The land, like a corpse, was stretched out in its burial linens, gray and sad and without memory.

(Amana washed dishes and dreamed about her daughter. She turned slowly in Mr. Fuller's kitchen, in a haze of steam and the smell of strong soap. Anxiously she looked forward to the day when Jemina would come back to Fort Benton, grown up and wise and strong. Amana's heart sang a strong song when she dreamed about all the good things that Jemina was learning in the unspoiled land of Canada.)

The axes ate the forest and licked its memories clean. And after this feast of axes there were only the piled bones of trees. A whole world blotted out and lost. All that the mighty trees had known, all that they had seen, the creatures that had lived among their branches, the endless summers that had shone through the boughs . . . all was lost. All the majesty of the land was lost.

(Amana blew out the lantern and closed her eyes.)

*   *   *

Jemina did not return to Fort Benton until she was fifteen years old. She greeted her mother with a charming smile. And then she excused herself and said she had a headache after the long journey.

Amana was delighted by Jemina. She had grown very

tall, and she was exceptionally handsome. She walked with grace and confidence. Amana exclaimed to Amalia, "Do you see how she has grown into a woman! Amalia, you were right! I was afraid of the school, but you were right!"

Then Amana went upstairs to bring Jemina a cup of tea made from an herb the grandmothers had taught her to use to cure headaches. She gently opened the bedroom door and was about to creep quietly to her daughter's side, when she was surprised to find Jemina talking excitedly to the women of the house.

"Jemina," Amana said, pleased, "how happy I am. You are feeling better already."

Jemina broke off her conversation when her mother came in.

"Please—please, *mamake-me* . . . my little one, don't stop. Don't stop talking. I want to listen. I want to know all about the school and what you have learned," Amana said with a gesture of pride, squeezing between the women so she could be close to her daughter.

Jemina smiled at her but did not speak. Amana crept silently toward the bed, looking intently at the young woman who was her daughter. She had changed so greatly that Amana could not easily recognize her. She spoke in the manner of British people, and she behaved strangely, as if she had memorized all that she said and did. Her dress was plain, but very similar to the dresses that were worn by the women in magazines. Her hair was piled upon her head. And she was wearing a little brooch on the high neckline of her blouse.

Adella said to Amana, "Listen to the marvelous things Jemina has been telling us! She has become a great lady! Just look at her, Miss Amana!"

Jemina fell back on the bed, pressing her fingers to her forehead. "Not now," she said. "I have a dreadful headache."

"Yes . . . yes," Amana murmured, offering the tea to her daughter, "she has come a very long way, and we must let her sleep."

"I got something from the chemist, Mother. That tea won't do any good. I just need to take a nap."

"Yes . . . yes, we must leave her so she can sleep. Rest, my little one. Just rest in your mama's big bed. You must leave everything to me. I will unpack your clothes. I have already made room in my closet. You must rest. Then you will feel better. Drink just a little bit of the tea. Believe your mother, it is good medicine. And it will take your headache away better than anything the chemist gave you."

"Just put the cup down, Mother. You mustn't treat me like a baby. I'll take a nap, and then I'll put my own things away. Adella has asked me to share her room with her, and she has an extra bureau just for me."

"But, Jemina . . ." Amana said, "I have arranged everything so you can stay here with me just like you did when you were a little girl."

Jemina avoided her mother's eyes. "I don't want to intrude on your privacy, Mother. So I told Adella I'd stay in her room."

"But there is plenty of room here," Amana insisted.

"But the bed . . ." Jemina said apologetically. "Mother, I'm too big to sleep with my mother anymore."

Amana looked at her daughter.

"It is all right, Jemina," she said. "You will not have to sleep with me. I have put down my old couch and backrests. I prefer an Indian mat to a bed."

Jemina glanced at her mother. Then she sat on the edge of the bed and said, "Oh, Mother, isn't that just like you! Here you have a nice home that Amalia has furnished with all these beautiful things so you can live like proper people, and you want to spoil it all by setting up that old Indian couch!"

Amana smiled. "You will be an Indian, Jemina," she said softly, "whether you sleep on a bed or on the floor."

"You forget, Mother," Jemina answered resentfully, "that my father was Jean-Pierre Bonneville from Montreal!"

"*Aih*, I had almost forgotten," Amana whispered. She looked at this stranger who was her daughter, trying to find something familiar in her eyes. "There are those of us who want to be one thing and there are those who want to be something else," Amana said solemnly, taking her daughter's hand and turning it over slowly. "That is how the world is, Jemina. There are those who make things and there are those who only know how to use them. And that is how it is for us. Some create new things while others cannot see things until someone else has made them. From the time you were born it has been like that, Jemina. I wish to be one person and you want to be someone else. So perhaps you are right, after all. Perhaps you are really the daughter of Jean-Pierre Bonneville and not the daughter of Amana. But tell me, Jemina—is the person you have become someone real, or is she somebody you have seen in a magazine?"

Suddenly Jemina sobbed. She shook with pain and confusion, and she wept. The women withdrew from the room in silence as Jemina, in desperation, fell into her mother's lap and urgently hugged her. "I don't know . . ." Jemina sobbed. "I don't know who I am anymore, Mama. I want something I can't explain."

"*Aih*, it will be good for you, little one," Amana chanted softly as she rocked Jemina in her arms. "It will be a good life. So don't cry anymore. I must be who I am, and you must try to find out who you are. And eventually it will be all right. We live in so many worlds, little one. It is confusing for me. And it is also confusing for you. But eventually we will all come to understand who it is that we truly are."

They rocked gently to and fro until the music of the Deluxe Talking Machine was silent at last and the girls went to their rooms and turned down their lamps and went to bed. Finally, when the moon made its way over the bleak little town and the voices of drunken men vanished into the distance, Amalia came quietly into the room and helped Amana lift the sleeping Jemina into the bed.

Then the two old friends looked at one another and

silently went down to the dark parlor, where they sat in Turkish leather rockers and watched the moon move over the squat, square, naked houses of Fort Benton.

"I have been feeling sorry for myself," Amana murmured. "But I should feel sorry for Jemina. I have had a dream while she has had nothing. She was born into a dead land. There is no center. The world in which we once lived and into which we brought our children is gone."

*　　*　　*

A few days later, the man from the government came to the door of Chez Amalia and demanded to see Amana. Jemina had just come home, but already the church-women of Fort Benton were indignant. They marched through the door, following the government agent into the parlor, glaring with disapproval at Adella when she asked them what they wanted.

"Our business is with the Indian woman who is the mother of this child," the official insisted.

"Well, for starters you'd do well to mind your own business—the whole lot of you! And for a second—" Adella shouted.

But Amana gestured for silence as she came into the parlor and confronted the strangers with dignity.

"I will speak to them," Amana murmured.

Still angry, Adella muttered an insult under her breath and sat down among the delegation.

"What do you want from me?" Amana asked.

Several of the women began to speak at once, but

the government official interrupted. "I have already told you that Indian children must attend the schools designated by the government. It is the law—"

Amana stepped toward the man with an expression so intense that it instantly silenced him. "No," she said in a strong voice. "It is not my law; it is your law. And Jemina is not your child; she is my child. I gave her life. I gave her breath. And I sent her to a good school and I paid much money for this."

The official began to respond, but Amana waved away his comment. "No!" she said again. "I am not listening now. I want things nice between us. I don't want trouble. But I am not listening to this talk. There are many children younger than my Jemina who are not at Indian school. But you care nothing for those children, who are hungry and cold and have no one to help them. You care for Jemina because she is here, in this house, this Chez Amalia! I say to you: No! I will not listen to lies. You care nothing for Jemina. You care only about the whores and the whorehouse! That is what bothers you and these women! But you lie. You say it is the law. You say you care for the education of Jemina. But all you care about is pride!"

"Madam!" the official exclaimed as the women shouted their indignation. "You have no right to use such language in the presence of Christian ladies!"

"Some Christians!" Adella said with a laugh.

Amana's expression became increasingly dark. "Now," she said with a flash of power coming into her eyes, "now you will go! And you will not come back again . . . not you and not these Christian ladies. My Jemina is a woman now. And I am a woman. I have lived through bad days and I have seen things you have never seen in your life. So much pain I have had. So much fear and death. Enough! No fear! No pain! You will not make pain and fear for us! So now you go and you do not come back to Chez Amalia!"

Intimidated, the official and his delegation stumbled toward the door. Adella laughed uproariously as they fled from the house. But Amana looked after them with an expression of dread.

"You scared them to death," Adella exclaimed with delight.

"*Aih,*" Amana murmured, "but that is not end of them."

She was right. Within the week the minister called at Chez Amalia.

"I have come to this blasphemous place because I know that you are a good woman," he told Amana. "I realize this is the only place where you can live. But surely it is not the sort of place where you want to bring up your daughter?"

Amana nodded respectfully. "These are my friends," she said quietly. "They have saved me from hunger and cold. They have been good to me for many years. They have shared everything with me. Why should I not want Jemina to live with them?"

The minister blushed and cleared his throat. For a

moment he was silent, and then he asked, "You know
what kind of place this is? Do you not realize what kind
of women these women are?"

Amana did not respond. She gently folded her arms
in her lap and gazed with curiosity at the minister.

"Good people turn away from these women. They
are damned. And everyone in this house is also damned.
Do you wanted your child to be damned?"

"*Aih*, I want good for Jemina. But I am confused.
Is my child damned for being here? Is my Jemina damned
because she stays at Chez Amalia? And if she is damned
for this, what of the many men who come here? You
do not turn from them. You do not say they are
damned."

Again the minister cleared his throat and pressed his
lips together.

"I come to you in peace," he said. "I come not to
criticize or to cause pain. I want to save you and your
daughter. That is my solemn duty. I want to lead you
from this dark house to a path of righteousness—the
true path of our Lord, Jesus Christ."

Amana nodded respectfully. *"Aih,"* she whispered,
"I am happy you come to Chez Amalia, because now
you see it is not such a bad place. The women here
are good and kind. And I thank you for the sympathetic
words you said to me. You are a good man . . . not
like government men."

The minister smiled warmly and touched Amana
on the shoulder. "Come to my church," he whispered

intensely. "If you and your daughter will come to see me at the parish house, we will pray together for your eternal souls. What joy you will know in the blood of our Lord! What a gift of salvation you will give to your daughter! Will you come to the church? Will you accept Jesus Christ as the Lord?" the minister pleaded.

Amana looked into the man's eyes and saw a rare gentleness there. A fragile smile passed over her lips.

Heartened, the minister continued with strong feeling. "Our Lord Jesus Christ," he said, "was born to bring salvation to all sinners. He is the light in the darkness. He is the Son of God, born immaculately of the Virgin. He gave his life that we might live."

Rapturously, the minister told Amana the story of Christ; of his birth and his life and his death on the cross. And when he had finished his remarkable tale, Amana nodded her head in amazement, deeply touched by the marvelous man named Jesus. When the minister saw this reverence in Amana's face, he became jubilant.

"And do you understand that Christ came into the world to save us?"

Amana nodded.

"And do you understand that he died on the cross for us?"

"*Aih,*" Amana murmured. "I do."

"Then," exclaimed the minister, "you believe in the true divinity of Jesus Christ and accept him as your Lord!"

Amana shook her head in confusion. "Oh," she said politely, "no, I do not believe, minister. It is you who believe in him."

The minister's face betrayed his disappointment. "I am sorry," Amana murmured, putting her hand on his shoulder. "I thought you understood. It is good that you believe in this marvelous story about Jesus. But it is your story; it is not mine. I do not have enough time in my life to understand your religion; and so I must try to understand my own."

*   *   *

> *I don't care, I don't care,*
> *If I do get mean and stony stares,*
> *If I'm never successful,*
> *It won't be distressful,*
> *'Cause I don't care!*

The Deluxe Talking Machine's tinny music filled the parlor. All the women were singing along with the new phonograph records that had just arrived from St. Louis.

"Wait a minutes . . . just wait for a minutes," Amalia announced in her booming voice, clearing a path to the talking machine with her elbows. "This is for sure the most important phonograph record I was ordered. So everybody is quiet and ready for the specialty song I am getting for celebrating Jemina's birthday! *Oui?*"

All the girls applauded, and Jemina squeezed Amana's hand and anxiously waited as Amalia put the new record on the gramophone.

I love you as I never loved before,
Since first I met you on the village green.
Come to me, or my dream of love is o'er.
I love you as I loved you
When you were sweet,
When you were sweet sixteen!

"Brava, Jemina!" Amalia shouted gaily, as the whores began to dance with one another, and Mr. Fuller puffed on his cigar and poured drinks.

"Isn't it marvelous!" Jemina exclaimed. "This winter when I was away from home on my birthday, I was so lonely! But it was worth waiting—just to celebrate it with you! Oh, Mama, I'm so happy!"

Amana nodded and watched as Jemina rushed among the swirling frocks.

"But no whiskey," Amana declared, "no whiskey for the child!"

All the women groaned and made faces at Amana, but she insisted, "No whiskey for Jemina! Do you hear what I say? Please be good friends and don't give the child any of that whiskey!"

"Here's to your belated sweet sixteen!" Adella shouted, tipping her glass to Jemina's lips and roaring with laughter as Amana tried to stop her. "Just one little sip won't hurt," the whores pleaded.

"Please, Mama," Jemina implored, "don't be angry on my birthday!"

Amana tried for a moment to hold firm, but Jemina

smiled at her and began to dance, twirling around until her dress lifted into the air and everyone applauded and laughed.

"*Vite! Vite, mes chères!*" Amalia boomed. "Hurry for getting to be ready, darlings. Monsieur Fuller is waiting for escorting all us for the circus as big surprise for Jemina!"

It was the first circus ever to come to Fort Benton. Ornately carved wagons, lumbering elephants, and a calliope piping merrily brought up the rear of the procession down Main Street. Glittering, silk-clad men and women on their horse-drawn floats flanked a marching band playing so loudly it was deafening. And all the colorfully costumed performers rode elegantly high, high above the crowd, while the clowns bounded along, making jokes and handing out leaflets.

"*Vite! Vite, mes chères!* Hurry, my darlings. We all going for big night at circus!"

The women were excited as they flocked around Mr. Fuller, who had bought enough tickets for the entire household. He winked proudly at Amalia and thrust his hands on her buttocks with a grin.

"*Mon Dieu!*" Amalia laughed as she took Amana's and Mr. Fuller's arms. "The *anniversaire de naissance, mon ami*, is for Jemina . . . not for me!"

The circus was one of the rustic little bands of performers that tried to imitate the grand shows of P. T. Barnum, traveling by rail throughout the territories and bringing entertainment to small towns. The marching band was playing "You're a Grand Old Flag," as men waved their hats in the air.

The entire town had turned out. Amana had never seen so many people. The wagons had been coming in from the cattle country for three days. There was a line from dawn till dusk at Mr. Fuller's restaurant. And hundreds of families were living in tents all around the circus grounds. There were even several automobiles honking noisily and chugging through the muddy streets.

Amana stared in every direction, amazed by the sights. She grasped Jemina's hand tightly, but Jemina was jumping into the air so she could see above the heads of the men lining the curb—trying to see the handsome young acrobats standing in elegant poses on top of the gilded circus wagons.

All the girls of Fort Benton were running after the wagons, waving to the performers. They rushed through the street with their brothers and escorts. Jemina wanted to be with them.

"Hello! Hello, Stella!" Jemina shouted to a girl whose father was a waiter at Mr. Fuller's restaurant. "Hello, Stella! Isn't it wonderful!"

But the girl ignored her and hurried past.

"Stella!" Jemina called, trying to catch up with the young woman as she joined her friends. Then, just as Jemina neared them, she heard Stella laughing.

"Hurry up before Jemina gets here!"

"Let's go!" another girl agreed. "My mother doesn't want me to have anything to do with her!"

"Well, no wonder." Stella giggled. "Her mother is black as midnight. Can you imagine, having a mother who washes dishes for a living!"

"There goes Miss Priss!" an Indian boy shouted as Jemina hurried back to Amana.

"They're just trash!" Jemina said. "All they are is Indian trash!"

Amana shook her head in dismay. "This is your special day . . . your birthday. Open your heart, child. You make your mother ashamed when you call your own people trash."

"They're not my people," Jemina muttered darkly. "My name is Jemina Bonneville. I'm just as white as any of them. I speak better English than they do, and I know about things they've never heard of!"

"Jemina!" her mother said. "You must not let them make you so unhappy! Be proud of both the Indian and the French in you."

But Jemina was still hurt and pulled away from her mother. She ran ahead toward Mr. Fuller, who led the procession of whores toward the circus tent.

"Jemina! Come back," Amana cried. But her daughter took Mr. Fuller's hand and would not look back at her mother. "*Aih,*" Amana sighed. She was vexed, but she understood her daughter's sorrow.

The band began to play "The Pineapple Rag," and everyone shouted and laughed as the townspeople poured into the big tent and scrambled for seats in the bleachers. Though Amana was sick at heart that Jemina did not want to be with her, she was content to see her daughter's face brighten with a smile as the ringmaster in his shiny top hat and tails came into the performing circle and began to announce the performers through his large red-and-white megaphone.

Amana sat silently beside Amalia and gazed dreamily as the splendid Arab horses pranced into the ring, trotting in a tight circle as they whinnied and pawed the air, their large eyes flashing with energy. The smell of horses brought back a remote sense of excitement and adventure. A sweet nostalgia flooded Amana's mind as the music played and the handsome horses trotted in perfect formation. Then a dark young man leaped onto the back of a huge white stallion and galloped out of the arena with a gallant wave of his arms. The crowd cheered and Jemina winced. She didn't particularly like the young horseman. "How did *he* ever get into the circus?" she asked Mr. Fuller, who laughed and said that all you needed to be in a circus was a head of wood and a good figure.

The crowd cheered so loudly that the young man was called back into the ring for an encore. He was very dark. Jemina decided that he was either a Negro or an Indian. She was glad when he finally bowed and rode out of the tent.

"That's one good-looking Indian!" Adella yelped in delight, slapping her hands together and laughing with approval. "Now that fella can come on up and see me any old time!"

"Such talk in front of the child!" Amana complained.

"Mon Dieu," Amalia exclaimed. "Tell me why should

I never find such mans when I am young girl instead for the stupid and weak knees I had for lover?"

All the women laughed heartily, but Mr. Fuller glanced with concern at Amana and Jemina. Then he too laughed. Amana shrugged and shook her head. "Such foolishness!" she grunted.

"Oh, Mother!" Jemina exclaimed, hugging Amana, "what a wonderful birthday you've given me!"

Tears crept into Amana's eyes. The love of her child and the rich strong scent of horses filled her with so much happiness and hope that she began to laugh and cry at the same time.

"Yes," she said, "it *is* a good birthday!"

And then the band began to play again and the aerialists paraded into the arena.

After the performance Mr. Fuller gave a party for Jemina at his restaurant. The women talked about nothing but the handsome young man in the circus.

"Did you ask?" Adella shouted again and again. "Mr. Fuller, did you find out his name?"

Mr. Fuller drew on his cigar with great nonchalance and was in no hurry to respond.

He stood and toasted Jemina's sixteenth birthday with a long florid speech about patriotism and purity and the virtues of innocence, which all the whores roundly booed, shouting humorous abuse at Mr. Fuller.

"In conclusion," he was saying, "I have taken the liberty of inviting a certain young man to join us for a drink."

All the women cheered. Mr. Fuller grinned and continued. "Some of you may be interested to know that his name is Mr. Ghost Horse—Mr. Jamie Ghost Horse. And he just happens to be that same lad who was getting so much applause this afternoon!"

Jamie Ghost Horse approached the table and bowed lavishly.

"Pleasure," he said with a theatrical manner. "Just delighted to meet up with all you very lovely ladies."

Jemina turned away. There was something about Jamie Ghost Horse that she resented. His airs. His elegant style. The way he spoke and moved. But her disapproval did not seem to matter to Jamie. He smiled at Jemina and said, "Now I'll just sit myself down right here next to the birthday girl!"

Again everyone laughed, and Jamie took his place at the table with an acrobatic flourish.

*   *   *

Amana decided that she liked Jamie Ghost Horse at once.

She liked his mocking arrogance. She liked the way he was proud of being Indian. She liked his sense of freedom and adventure. And so she was pleased when Jamie announced to the women of Chez Amalia that he was staying on in Fort Benton when the circus left town.

He often visited Chez Amalia, where he told stories of his travels. Amana loved to hear his strong voice, and was fascinated by the details of his exploits. There was something about this young man that made Amana happy. He made her feel proud of being an Indian, and he made her smile and laugh. He drank too much, and he liked to look at himself in the mirror in the parlor, but to Amana he was a rare survivor from the long-ago summers when Indian men were still story-tellers.

Amana watched Jamie Ghost Horse carefully when he sat in the parlor, drinking with the women and re-counting tales about growing up in the Great Smoky Mountains. His parents had been stars in the Buffalo Bill Wild West Show, and they had taken him with them all over the world.

"The Congress of Rough Riders of the World!—that's what they called us!" he exclaimed proudly. "Two electric plants! Two hundred and fifty thousand candle-power! That's brighter than daylight, ladies! Just imagine that—brighter than daylight!" he said with a wave of his arm. "Eighty-three thousand Englishmen bought tick-ets in just one day in London, England! And my folks were part of all that!"

He basked in the attention of his audience, talking for hours, telling jokes, and describing with exuberance the exciting cities he had visited.

His grandmother, he said, was a Cherokee "princess" from Georgia, and his grandfather was an escaped slave from Mississippi. "It's just 'cause I got the best of all possible races," he informed the whores in Amalia's par-lor, "that I turned out being such a damn fine-lookin' fella!"

Amana laughed. Not since the old days of hunters and warriors had she heard a man with such shameless pride. It pleased her greatly that Jamie Ghost Horse was putting on a fine show, for she suspected that he did it in part to impress Jemina. Amana had guessed, from the first moment Jamie had met Jemina, that these two young people were destined for one another. And so Amana smiled happily when Jemina crept into the doorway of the parlor and listened as Jamie Ghost Horse talked about his life.

"He is the only man who could make Jemina accept her Indian heritage," Amana thought when she saw Jemina cautiously move into the parlor.

"*Ah, bien!*" Amalia murmured to Amana. "Now she takes the bait."

The two old women watched as Jemina carefully took a seat next to Adella.

"Jemina and he both have spirit!" Amana whispered with a contented smile.

Amalia, however, was not convinced. "*Ma chère, peut être . . . peut-être,*" she said, shaking her head. "Unfortunate, my dear Amana, this daughter for you is having all your strength but none of your wisdom. *Mon Dieu!* . . . God help him if he marries her, *ma chère!*"

"But Amalia!" Amana objected. "She is a good girl. She just needs a strong husband who will make her give up all her airs."

"*Peut-être . . . peut-être . . .* perhaps," Amalia murmured.

So Amana and Amalia sat in the parlor and watched the two young people perform their complicated mating dance. And in the night, after the customers had gone home and while Mr. Fuller lingered quietly over his last whiskey, they would talk about Jamie and Jemina.

"Tell me something—how are you two old dragons planning to rope that poor Indian boy?" Mr. Fuller asked with a grin.

Amalia smiled. "I think it is a good time for inviting Jamie Ghost Horse for dinner."

"Yes!" Amana agreed.

"Jesus!" Mr. Fuller bellowed. "That guy doesn't have half a chance with two old warriors like you on his trail!"

And so a dinner was planned for just the five of them: Mr. Fuller, Amana, Amalia, and the two young people. Amalia stacked whiskey bottles on the sideboard. Mr. Fuller made a huge roast beef, and Jemina arranged the dining room table in the exacting British manner she had learned at Miss Wells' Girls' School.

On the evening of the dinner party, Jemina lingered in front of the mirror, gazing at the handsome gown her mother had ordered for her. She fastened a brooch at her neckline and smiled happily at her image, bowing deeply and turning so she could see her profile in the mirror.

"How *de-light-ful*, Mr. Ghost Horse, for you to join *notre petit repas*," she rehearsed as she turned in front of her reflection. Then she took a deep breath and opened the bedroom door. As she swept down the hallway toward the stairs, Adella stuck her head out of her bedroom. "Cheerio!" she whispered.

"I just have to make him like me," Jemina confided when she kissed Adella and hurried down the stairs.

"Tallyho!" the girls whispered as every door along the hallway opened and the whores waved to Jemina as she descended.

*   *   *

The dinner was a great success. The roast beef was medium rare, and the whiskey was strong and abundant. Amalia was aglow in her best gown from Paris and a little hat with a veil. Amana had plaited her gray hair in two long, ermine-decorated braids. She had only one dress, a plain black one with a big skirt and a narrow collar, but she pressed it carefully, and then she unwrapped her wedding moccasins, which she kept in the trunk in her room, and put them on for the first time since the day she had gone to live with Far Away Son when she had been in her twelfth winter. They still fit. The sight of the magnificent little moccasins that her sister, SoodaWa, had made for her brought tears to her eyes, and for a long time she sat silently on the floor before the trunk as ghosts and shadows came and went in a strong current of memory.

After dinner, Mr. Fuller excused himself early, bidding the two young people good night.

Jamie Ghost Horse was telling a story about the Milas Family Troupe of Aerialists. So he just nodded to Mr.

Fuller, without pausing in his narration. "Well," he continued enthusiastically, "they were a fantastic act from the city of Athens in Greece! And their son, Alexander, was just about my own age, and we became good friends when my folks were working with the circus in Paris, France! Anyway, old man Milas, he went and asked me if I had a mind to be an aerialist. 'Cause, he said, y'know, that I had a fine body and lots of muscles and all. He said I would make a great flier—which is the one that flies through the air, you see, instead of the other one that hangs by his knees from the trapeze and catches the fliers. Old man Milas said I'd make a terrific partner for his son, Alexander. And, can you imagine? I learned how to do all that stuff in just a couple of months, and I became part of the Milas family. I even learned how to speak Greek! *Kali mera! Efcharisto. . . . Bira. . . . Krasi aspro!* How d'you like that!"

"*Alors!*" Amalia gasped. "Do you see that—he can speaking the Greek!"

"Well," Jemina said mischievously, "a few words of it anyway."

Jamie Ghost Horse shot Jemina a dark look and then continued his story. "Well, like I said, I joined the world-famous Milas Family Troupe of Aerialists! And don't think it wasn't hard, 'cause I had to work myself to death to figure out all those dangerous tricks. Don't forget, I'm just a cowboy. I can do absolutely anything on a horse, but this work was way up in the air in all them bright lights! The first time I tried it—even with a harness—I tell you I like to piss my pants!" He hooted merrily. "Uh, that is . . ." he added self-consciously, "if the ladies know what I mean."

Amalia laughed boisterously, and then she said, "You are perfect gentleman, Mr. Ghost Horse . . . *parfait!* And so, if you make a little funny now and then, I think it not so bad."

Reassured, Jamie lit up with greater confidence. "Well," he exclaimed, standing and lavishly taking off his jacket, "that's how I got all these muscles in my shoulders and arms, y'see. Swinging way up there in all them lights! With all them folks watching . . . all the kids and gentlemen . . . and *all* them pretty ladies!" he said with a big smile as he strode around the parlor in his shirt sleeves.

"*Parfait!*" Amalia announced in a big voice. "*Quel homme! Oui, ma chère*, Jemina. . . . this is some real man!"

"Goodness!" Jemina exclaimed as she looked at Jamie Ghost Horse. "Put on your jacket. Gentlemen don't sit around in their shirt sleeves—showing off for everyone!"

"Jemina!" Amana admonished.

But Jemina could not be silent. The words tumbled out. "What nonsense!" she shouted as she glared at Jamie. "Mr. Fuller manages to keep his jacket on when he is with ladies—even in the heat of summer! That's just plain good manners. Anybody who's a gentleman knows that!"

"Says who?" Jamie retorted angrily.

"I say!" Jemina exclaimed.

"And what the hell does a sixteen-year-old know about manners?" he shouted.

"I know how a gentleman is supposed to act around ladies!" Jemina shouted.

"You wouldn't know a gentleman if you had one sitting in your lap!" Jamie muttered.

"Mr. Fuller is a gentleman. That much I know for certain. And as for you, Jamie Ghost Horse, you're just an ignorant Indian trying to be somebody you're not and never will be!"

"Well, let me tell you something! If you'll excuse me for speaking plain, Mr. Fuller ain't no gentleman by a long shot! He runs a little restaurant in this cow town!"

"Oh, Amalia, tell him to be quiet!" Jemina exclaimed.

"But me," Jamie continued, "now I'm a real gentleman. I don't run any little restaurant. What I run is my own life. So you stop worrying, Jemina Bonneville, about my jacket and just worry about yourself and who you really are."

Jemina angrily gathered her skirts as she stood up, and glared at Jamie Ghost Horse before running upstairs, shouting, "You bully! You no-count Indian bully!"

"And you," he shouted after her, "you're like some silly Southern belle! All full of fancy airs even though you've never been anywhere and you don't know anything! You don't even know what the real world is all about! And you forget that you're part Indian yourself!''

Suddenly he stopped yelling. A look of distress came over his face as he turned slowly to Amana.

"I'm sorry, ma'am, but your daughter can really get my goat. I guess the way I carried on, I'd better go now," he said sheepishly.

Amana smiled faintly and put her hands on the young man's shoulders. And then, after gazing at him, she softly kissed his forehead. "It's those we like that we get angry with," she said. "You come again."

*   *   *

The hour was late, and most of the women of the house had already gone upstairs with their gentlemen. Adella sat with a forlorn expression, holding Amalia's hand.

"I just hate this time of night," she murmured.

Amalia did not respond. She dozed in the rocking chair, a contented smile on her lips.

"I always get feeling sad when it's late and the house is quiet," Adella said. "But it never seems to bother you," she added shyly, glancing admiringly at Jamie Ghost Horse.

He emptied his glass and grinned. "I sorta like it," he said as he put another record on the gramophone. "The soft music. All the empty chairs. It's peaceful, don't you think? Like all your troubles have gone to bed and there's nothing left to bother you."

Amana grunted softly as she stood up and roused Amalia. "For us it is time to go to bed with our troubles," she murmured. "Come along, Amalia—you will have a bad back again if you spend the whole night in that chair. Come, *chère amie*, it is time for us to take our old bodies upstairs."

"Good night," Jamie Ghost Horse said as Amana and Amalia nodded to him. "I'll see myself out."

"No need to leave," Amana told him. "You stay as long as you like, and just make yourself comfortable."

"I appreciate it, ma'am; 'cause that room of mine over at the hotel ain't nothing by comparison to Chez Amalia."

Amana smiled and gazed at Jamie Ghost Horse. "It's good to have you here. So just make yourself at home." And then she added, "Are you coming, Adella?"

Reluctantly, with one last glance at Jamie, Adella followed the old women upstairs.

Jamie lit a cigar and filled his glass, and then he walked very slowly around the parlor, daydreaming about nothing in particular as he listened to the tinny waltz that came from the gramophone. He nodded his head to the rhythm, and then gradually his feet picked up the beat and he extended his arms to an imaginary partner and began to glide to the music.

When he heard someone laugh, he quickly turned to the door, where Jemina stood smiling.

"Don't be cross," she insisted, coming into the room. "I wasn't laughing at you. I just never knew that men ever danced all by themselves like that."

"Well, they do," he said with embarrassment. "Now you know."

"Let's not argue. Please . . ." she whispered as she sat down. "Let's not argue anymore."

"That's fine with me."

They fell into an awkward silence.

"I didn't know you liked to dance," Jemina said softly.

"I used to go dancing all the time," he said, puffing on his cigar. Then he became conscious of the smoke and quickly put it out. "Sorry."

"Please don't stop smoking on my account," she said. "You were having such a good time. I feel as if I've intruded."

"Hell, Jemina, it's your house."

They fell silent once again.

"Where did you go dancing?" Jemina finally asked him.

"What's that?"

"You said you used to go dancing all the time. . . ."

"Oh, yeah—well, all over the world. I fairly danced myself around the world!"

"In Europe?" Jemina softly asked.

"You bet your life! In Paris and London and Berlin. I even danced in New York City and New Orleans and Chicago! Like I told you, I near to danced myself around the whole world one time or another."

"Do you know something?" Jemina said.

"What's that?" he asked cautiously.

"I know I shouldn't say it, but you do an awful lot of bald-faced bragging, Jamie Ghost Horse."

"Well, there you go again. I never knew anybody who had a harder time being nice!"

Jemina laughed. "I was only joking," she insisted.

"Like hell you were," he snorted.

"Honest to goodness . . . that's just the way I am."

Jamie sighed in resignation and relit his cigar with a broad gesture of defiance. Then he put another record on the gramophone and said, "Well, if that's the way you are and we're not going to argue, there's not much else for us to do."

"Yes there is," Jemina whispered.

"Like what?" he challenged. "What would you like to do?"

"I'd like to dance," she said softly.

Jamie Ghost Horse paused a long moment. Then gradually he smiled broadly. "Well, great balls of fire, why the hell didn't you say so in the first place!"

He nodded his head to the music, and then his feet picked up the rhythm, and he took Jemina in his arms and they began to turn around and around to the waltz that filled the parlor.

PART
III

What is unknown and unthought
By mankind
Wanders in the night
Through the labyrinth of the heart.

GOETHE

FOUR

It was in the winter that Jemina changed into Mrs.
Jamie Ghost Horse.

Amana was delighted. Yet on the day that the minister
came to the parlor of Chez Amalia, it seemed to her
that something was wrong. Who was this curious man
in the black suit? Who was this minister . . . this holy
man who was not a holy man?

In the night Amana had dreamed of lovers. She had
dreamed of Jean-Pierre Bonneville. She had seen the
beautiful black eyes of Yellow Bird Woman—eyes full
of love. Amana's dreams were filled with the sound of
flutes. But the morning resounded with the grim lamen-
tation of the broken fields, the ghosts of trees, the call
of birds lost in an unfamiliar sky.

Amana came slowly down the stairs, staring off into
the empty air, seeing things that other people could
not see. She watched Jemina from the stairs, suddenly
afraid that her daughter might forever wind around herself like a dust devil, going nowhere . . . and nowhere
again.

As the women of the house circled Jemina and flattered her, as they rustled in and out of the room in their fine dresses, Amana recalled the winter of starvation and how her emaciated child fought for life in those dark days when Jean-Pierre Bonneville had deserted her.

Amana wanted to be happy. She wanted to be grateful for the good fortune of her daughter and for her strong and handsome groom, but at night love and fear merged in her dreams, and she could not escape the feeling of dread with which she awakened. It sometimes seemed to Amana that her daughter's spirit was filled with a conflict that left little room for anything else. She longed for Jemina to be happy. But she wondered if she had been wrong in pushing Jamie and Jemina together. She wondered if her daughter loved Jamie, or if she really loved anyone. Was she marrying him just because everyone else wanted her to and because she didn't know what else to do with her life?

The gramophone sang its metallic song. To Amana it was a curious wedding music that came from the mouth of a machine. But Jemina was to be married by the white man's minister and to the white man's music. She did not know the ceremonies of Indian weddings. So Amana sang under her breath in honor of her child.

> *When the earth was made,*
> *When the first sky dawned,*
> *When my first song was heard,*
> *Then the holy mountain leaned toward me*
> *With life.*

Amana chanted to herself as she descended the stairs.

> *The day broke with slender rain,*
> *And the voice of thunder spoke*
> *Four times.*
> *When the earth was made*
> *And the first sky dawned,*
> *Then my first song*
> *Woke the daughter in my womb.*
> *My singing breathed life*
> *Into her spirit,*
> *And she was born of the wind.*

Jemina caught sight of her mother.

"Mama!" she exclaimed while Amalia frantically stitched one last silk flower on the wedding dress. "Stop singing and tell Amalia to finish! She has been sewing on this dress for weeks—and now she's at it again, Mama! I'll still be standing here when the ceremony starts! Mother, tell her to finish it fast! Amalia, please finish my dress or I'll never get to marry Jamie Ghost Horse!"

"The dress is not important, Jemina," Amana intoned in a colorless voice. "You will marry Jamie Ghost Horse even if your dress is not finished. He is different from anyone you know, and you want things you don't understand. He gets the attention you have always wanted. So you will marry him."

Jemina tossed her head. "That's right," she exclaimed petulantly. "And then maybe I'll get away from this terrible town at last!"

"And from me," Amana added sadly. "You will also get away from me at last."

"Ah!" Amalia cried. "She is only nervous! You must forgive her, *ma chère!*"

Amana shook her head and the three women urgently embraced each other, weeping.

"I am an old woman," Amana whispered to Jemina. "There is nothing left for me but the past. And for you there is no past. There is only the future."

"Come . . . come, *ma chère,*" Amalia pleaded, "let us not make unhappy such important day!"

"I love you," Amana murmured as she gently touched Jemina's face. "Sometimes I want too much from you. I don't know why it is, but I dream that you will bring back all the days that are gone."

Jemina hugged her mother. "It is my wedding day, Mama. Please try—"

"*Aih,*" Amana continued, "it is your wedding day and I cannot help remembering the men I once loved and how distant they have become."

"But I want you to be happy for me, Mama. I know you want me to get married, and I know you like Jamie. So I don't understand why you are so unhappy."

"I am unhappy, my child, because I am like my grandmothers of many years ago. I sometimes think that I have lived too long. I have seen too many good people die and all our traditions disappear, leaving nothing. I cannot let go of the old days and I cannot find any happiness in the new days."

"Ah," Amalia pleaded, "you must try to be happy for the marriage of your child!"

Amana shook her head and could not speak. She kissed Jemina's hands and gazed urgently into her face, looking for something that was not there. And then silently she returned to her room, where she sat on the floor with her dress billowing up around her in the wind that blew in through the open windows, and in the gust came countless yellow butterflies and the faces of Far Away Son and Jean-Pierre Bonneville. And in the frigid air came the voice of her sister, SoodaWa, calling out to her: "Come away!"

And so in the winter the minister came to the parlor of Chez Amalia, and while the girls hugged one another and Amalia played the organ from Sears, Roebuck, Mr. Fuller gave away the bride, and Jemina turned into Mrs. Jamie Ghost Horse. And Amana wept.

*   *   *

That spring, Jemina and Jamie packed their belongings and gave up the sunny room Amalia had given them for their honeymoon.

"If we're going to get to St. Louis in time to rejoin the circus," Jamie explained, "we'll have to catch tomorrow's boat for sure."

That evening Jemina came into Amana's room and silently sat on the bed next to her mother.

"Mama," she whispered.

Amana looked at her, filled with remorse and love. They had not often spoken since the wedding day. And the pain that accompanied the meeting of their eyes was so intense that neither woman could bear it.

"Mama," Jemina murmured again.

Amana looked at Jemina. "Can it be that nothing of value remains in the world?" she thought. And how could she blame her daughter for being a stranger in a strange world? *"Aih,"* Amana sighed as she kissed her daughter just once.

"Mama," Jemina whispered as tears streamed down her cheeks.

"When I became the wife of the old man called Far Away Son, I had lived only twelve winters," Amana said. "But inside me was a river of history that flowed like a torrent from my grandmothers and from their grandmothers before them. Now the river does not flow. It has become like a woman who can no longer bring forth children. I am that woman. I am that river. And you, Jemina, you are a land without memory. You are a woman without a river. You are something so new that we do not yet have a name for you. Yet one day you will have children who will hunger for the past. What will you tell them? What will you give them to quench their thirst for memory? You must do more than survive. You are a warrior as I was once a warrior, but you do not know what you are fighting for. When I was young I fought for the freedom to become myself— but you do not know who it is you wish to be. Forgive me, Jemina—I am too old to fight for your freedom. You must fight for it yourself."

Jemina did not know what to say.

For a long time Amana remained silent, and then she whispered, "He is a simple boy. He wants to be someone special, Jemina. Try not to ask too much from him. Do you understand? Be good to him."

The mother and daughter gazed silently at one another. Then with a sob Jemina embraced Amana. "Mama!" she cried wildly as she sprang to her feet and rushed toward the door.

And then Jemina was gone.

*   *   *

In the evening Mr. Fuller chugged up in front of Chez Amalia in his new Model T Ford and took Amana and Amalia for a ride down the road and across the wide, open fields, guzzling whiskey and shouting while the ladies' parasols bobbed in the amber light of sunset. On other occasions Mr. Fuller would take his two old friends to the picture show, where Mary Pickford always brought great tears to Amalia's eyes. Amana gazed silently at the strange shadow people and wondered if one day all the people of the world might turn into shadows upon a screen.

Once a week, when a postcard came from Jemina and Jamie, Mr. Fuller would put on his spectacles, clear his throat, and then read the brief messages to Amana and Amalia. The little notes scribbled on the backs of the pictures told Amana about a world completely different from Fort Benton. Amana would listen to Mr. Fuller as he read the words, and she would smile, and when he had finished, she always asked him to read the words once again.

Every month a money order for two dollars arrived for Amana from Jamie Ghost Horse. And sometimes there was a package containing a gift: a plaster cast of the Statue of Liberty, a bronze piggy bank, a necklace of cut-glass beads, or a photograph of President Taft. Amana turned these objects over slowly in her wrinkled hands.

Fort Benton was becoming a large town with electric lights and streetcars. Mr. Fuller was getting old. He hired a black man with green eyes to do the cooking at the restaurant. And Amana now worked at the cash register.

"Washing dishes isn't a proper job for a lady like you, Miss Amana," Mr. Fuller told her one day. So Amana collected money from the customers and pressed the keys of the register and put the coins in the little drawer. She sat behind the cash register and stared off into the empty air, seeing things that others could not see. She saw flowers bloom from the telephone poles and she saw a cascade of lavender butterflies rain down upon the mud-filled street where misty animals with human faces drifted like smoke among the wildly charging carriages and automobiles.

Many Blackfeet boys were volunteering for the army. And the women of Fort Benton were selling Liberty Bonds. The post office was filled with posters, and the radio in the parlor of Chez Amalia asked everyone to help America win the Great War. But for Amana all the wars had ended long ago.

Calf Woman had only one son by Louis Perkins. The boy was eighteen years old when he went off with the army to a place in Belgium called Ypres. There he was blinded by poison gas. Calf Woman called Amana on the telephone in the parlor, and the two old women wept together for Calf Woman's blinded son.

"What is this war for?" Calf Woman cried bitterly.

"I do not know . . . I do not know," Amana said into the telephone. "My friend, I cannot tell you because I do not know what it is for."

Each day Amana understood less about the world around her. Each day she found herself at a greater distance from the people in the streets and in Mr. Fuller's Fine Restaurant. She was becoming invisible and mute. No one noticed her. Gradually, she faded into the ground like a silent rain.

Then one morning, Amana got a letter. It was from Calf Woman. Amana knew it was from her old friend because she could smell the bit of sweetgrass that Calf Woman had put into the pink envelope. The reservation schoolteacher had written down the words for Calf Woman just as she had spoken them.

Amana shook her head with impatience, for she could not understand the scratching on the paper. She had to wait for Mr. Fuller so he could read the letter to her. At last, when he came through the door, Amana rushed to him with the letter. But despite her prodding,

he slowly hung up his hat and coat, saying "Ahuh . . .
ahuh . . . let's see . . . let's see what your friend has
to say. . . ."

Amana blinked her eyes expectantly and touched her
fingertips to her lips as Mr. Fuller methodically put on
his glasses and began to read:

*"Hugh Monroe passed on last week. There was nobody but
me and Reverend Welch at the burial. Hugh worked in the
mines till he was sixty-eight. Then he stayed home with all
the money he made scratching at the earth in the dark. Well,
now he is gone. Rest in peace. And I thought you should know,
Amana, because it turns out that he loved you. That's exactly
what he told Louis Perkins when they were out drinking one
night. He always loved you, he said. Broke his heart to see the
way Jean-Pierre Bonneville deserted you. Wanted to marry you
but never had the courage to ask, I guess. So now he is gone."*

At the bottom of the letter was the mark that Calf
Woman made on the page.

Amana took the letter into her hands and slowly
crushed it. She blew her nose in her large handkerchief.
Then she shook her head and moved her lips silently.
Mr. Fuller watched her, but he did not speak. *"Aih,"*
whispered Amana as she went back to her place behind
the cash register.

That night the Great War in Europe ended and the
proprietors closed their shops. Everyone got drunk. The
sky was full of rockets, but to Amana it seemed as if
the stars were dying in a shower of agony.

*   *   *

It was not until a few years later that Jemina gave birth to her first child.

Amana received a postcard for New Year's Eve. It had a picture on it of the Grand Hotel in Sioux City, Idaho. "Blessed event expected any day!" was scribbled in Jamie's large handwriting. That was all the card said.

Amana was so nervous that she asked Mr. Fuller to call the Grand Hotel on the telephone in the parlor, but when he finally got through to the hotel, the clerk told him the circus people had already checked out.

"And you better tell them circus folks to stay out of Sioux City!" the man shouted over the telephone. "The whole bunch of them lammed out of here without paying the bill!"

"Well," Mr. Fuller said apologetically, "don't you know there's a depression on? Makes it tough on show business people just like it does on all the rest of us!"

"Ask him where they went," Amana insisted, tugging at Mr. Fuller's sleeve. "Ask him where Jemina and Jamie went!"

"It's no good," Mr. Fuller said, " 'cause that hothead went and hung up on me!"

"*Mon Dieu!*" Amalia exclaimed as she paced back and forth in the parlor. "Where could he have gone without any money and with a pregnant wife? What is the matter for that foolish fellow? I thought he told us he had too much money. They always writing about all the big money he is making! *Mon Dieu, quelle catastrophe!*"

"They will be all right," Amana whispered to her friend. "I know that everything is going to be all right.

It just has to be all right!" Amana insisted desperately. "Because this child is going to bring something good back into the world! This baby is going to carry within him all the good days that have vanished . . . all the legend days! All things will be born again with him!" Amana exclaimed. Then suddenly a look of terror flooded into her face. "But who is looking after Jemina!"

"Now both of you best calm down," Mr. Fuller said as he poured himself some whiskey. "You better sit yourself down and relax before you make a nervous wreck out of me. That's what you two ought to do, 'cause there's no good in getting all upset about something you can't fix."

"*Taisez-vous! Taisez-vous, chère amie, s'il vous plaît!* Just be quiets!" Amalia stammered. "Ah, *quelle catastrophe!* . . . No moneys and the wife is eight months pregnant! What kind of monkey around is this?"

"Amalia!" Amana cried. "I don't want Jemina to have her baby in a strange place! I want her to have it here in the house. Amalia, I'm afraid what will happen to the child if they let the white doctors bring it into the world!"

"Now . . . now . . . now," Mr. Fuller insisted. "You two had just better settle down. The both of you are getting out of hand. In a few days I bet you we get a telephone call or maybe even a telegram from Jamie."

But there was no word from Jamie Ghost Horse. It seemed as if he and Jemina had simply vanished. At first Mr. Fuller was reassuring, but as the days passed without any word from Jamie, he too became concerned and placed calls all over the country, trying to find somebody in show business who knew where the circus people had gone.

But no one knew anything about Jamie and Jemina.

Amana pulled the window blinds of her room and sat in the darkness, chanting to Sun. And Amalia knelt in the parlor in front of the little cross on the wall, whispering, *"Ave Maria, gratia plena. . . ."*

Amalia's urgent prayer intermingled with Amana's droning song, *"E-spoom-mo-kin-on . . ."* like distant thunder filled with rain.

But still there was no word from Jamie.

Amana could hear the voice of the child calling to her in the distant thunder. She could hear the soft pulsing heart of her unborn grandchild. And she wept more bitterly than she had wept when Jemina was born on a wind-filled, lonely night long ago.

Finally the telephone rang.

"Hello, Mama," Jemina's voice came through the telephone. "It's a little boy, Mama."

Her voice sounded so tired that Amana interrupted, "Are you all right, Jemina? Is everything all right?"

"Sure . . . sure, Mama, everything's fine."

"And Jamie?" Amana questioned urgently. "Is he all right?"

"He's fine."

"And the baby . . . is the baby all right, Jemina?"

"Yes, he's fine, Mama. He cries day and night, but he's fine."

Then there was a silence.

"Listen, Mama," Jemina said, "we're coming on home. As soon as we can catch a train, we're coming on back there for a while. Is that okay, Mama?"

Amana nodded her head as tears flowed into her eyes.

"Are you there, Mama?"

"Yes . . . yes, I'm here."

"I said . . . is it okay for us to come back there for a while?"

"Yes . . . yes," Amana murmured. "You just come back home to us, Jemina. All three of you come home as quickly as you can."

"Okay, Mama. We'll be there in a week or two."

"Do you need any money, Jemina?" Amana murmured.

"Thank you, Mama! If you could have Mr. Fuller send us about twenty-five dollars, it would sure help."

The tears flowed from Amana's eyes. "Yes," she said, "I will send money today. I will send money. Tell me where to send it. I will have Mr. Fuller send it off to you right away."

One of the girls came to the phone and took down the address with her eyebrow pencil. Then Amana quickly took the receiver back and said, "Today, for sure, I will send money."

"Thanks, Mama. . . ."

"Is the baby really all right, Jemina?"

"Yes, honest to God, Mama, he's just fine."

"What do you call him? What are you calling your first son, Jemina?"

"He's called . . . Reno."

"But what does that mean, Jemina? What does Reno mean?"

"It doesn't mean anything, Mama. It's just a name."

Amana shook her head in confusion. For a moment she stammered into the telephone, hoping to say something encouraging to her daughter. But Jemina said, "Good-bye, Mama."

*   *   *

"There's no money in the circus anymore," Jamie complained as he slouched on the couch in the parlor of Chez Amalia with Mr. Fuller. "All the big acts are gone. The circus is just a two-bit business now . . . playing a lot of hick towns for nickels and dimes. The real money isn't in the circus anymore—it's in the follies and all those George M. Cohan shows back in New York City."

Amana sat in the parlor listening and watching Jamie. His face was puffy and haggard. He kept playing with a button on his jacket while he tossed down whiskey as fast as Mr. Fuller could pour it. He had gained weight. His belly was starting to roll over his belt, and his youth and good looks had vanished.

Amana sat watching her son-in-law and daughter as she held the child named Reno, and she could feel his heart beating against her body. She gently rocked the baby as she gazed at her daughter and recalled the tiny infant of that winter of starvation. She remembered how she had kept Jemina alive with her own vomit. Now Jemina was the mother of this new child who slept in Amana's arms.

"Well," Mr. Fuller said in a sympathetic tone, "sure is sad the way things turned out for you, Jamie. It's tough for everybody these days . . . with the depression and all . . . but we sorta figured from your postal cards that things wasn't so bad in the show business."

Jamie did not answer. He glanced self-consciously at Amana and downed another whiskey.

"Yeah," Mr. Fuller repeated to fill the awkward silence, "we just figured you was doing nicely from all them postal cards."

"Well, y'know how it is," Jamie murmured, "no sense in worrying you folks with our problems. We did the best we could. But then the Crash really messed us up."

"If you were doing so well," Mr. Fuller insisted, "how come you never saved a nest egg for a rainy day?"

Jamie sighed and shook his head with resignation. "How's anybody supposed to save money when Jemina spends it faster than you can make it?" he said glumly.

"Oh, that's right. It's all my fault!" Jemina exclaimed, coming into the parlor in her bathrobe.

"I thought you were going to sleep all day!" Jamie snapped, giving his wife a black look.

"So you can sit down here getting good and drunk and telling lies about me!" Jemina snorted.

"Oh, to hell with you," Jamie rumbled, picking up his coat. "I'm going for a walk!"

"Well, just see you don't walk over to the bar and spend all that money Amana gave you, y'hear! That money isn't just for you! You hear me, mister?" Jemina shouted after him.

"I'm sorry," Jemina said, turning to her mother, "I can't believe a word Jamie says anymore. One day he comes from North Carolina and the next day he's supposed to be from Georgia or Kentucky or who knows where!"

Mr. Fuller frowned and looked at Amana, who nodded but would not speak.

"You remember how he used to tell about meeting the Milas Family Troupe in Paris?" Jemina said. "And how the son, Alexander, talked the Milas family into letting Jamie join their act? You remember all those lies?"

"Well, sure, I remember," Mr. Fuller said.

"All those lies . . ." Jemina muttered. "Even I learned *something* about show business, and I can tell you this: the Milas troupe was a real headliner! I mean they were a top attraction, making all kinds of money. So you tell me this—how come Jamie ended up in a third-rate circus if he performed with the Milas troupe?"

"What difference does it make now?" Amana asked quietly.

"It makes a lot of difference," Jemina insisted, lighting a cigarette. "It makes a whole lot of difference to me!" she exclaimed angrily. " 'Cause he told me lies. He was so grand. He was so popular. I thought we were really going somewhere. That's what I thought! But what did

I know? Now just take a look at him. He's drinking himself to death, and I can't stand another minute of it!'' Jemina sobbed, biting her lip and shaking with rage.

"Well," Mr. Fuller sighed, "perhaps Jamie is gonna have to look around for some kind of job and settle down now that you've got the baby and all."

"The baby!" Jemina echoed sadly.

Mr. Fuller edged from his seat and excused himself. "Believe me, Jemina," he said timidly as he was leaving the parlor, "I sure hope things work out for all of you. But y'know, I promised Amalia to be down at the dock with the Model T, cause she's gonna have lots of stuff she bought for the spring ball."

Then he quickly left the mother and daughter alone.

"Now don't start with me, Mama," Jemina whispered defensively. "I know what you're thinking, but just don't start with me, 'cause I've taken about all I can take."

Amana saw the sadness in Jemina's face. She strapped the baby to her back and approached her daughter slowly. With a hesitant hand she touched Jemina on the shoulder. "It will be all right," she said. "I am old, but I am still a strong woman. I will make everything good for you again, Jemina."

Jemina sobbed uncontrollably and grasped her mother's hand. "I'm sorry," she wept. "Really, Mama . . . I'm sorry that we are such failures!"

Amana smiled encouragingly and pressed her fingers gently against her daughter's shoulder. "No, you have not failed. You have left the things of the spirit unnoticed. You have forgotten how to look at the world, Jemina."

"But I wanted to change everything! I thought I could do it."

"What, Jemina? What did you want to change, child?"

"Oh, I don't know. I wanted my life to be beautiful like Miss Wells told us it would be. I thought I could get out of this awful house and this awful town! I thought I would have a big home somewhere nice, and then I could take you in so you wouldn't have to work all your life and so you could have some nice dresses and somewhere decent to live where everybody doesn't hate us just because we're what we are."

"And what are we, Jemina?" her mother gently asked.

But Jemina would not answer the question. She wiped away her tears. "When I look at Jamie, I see my own failure, Mama, and I can't bear looking at the way things have turned out!"

Once again Jemina wiped away her tears.

"Mama, please don't be mad at me. I hate to ask you," she said, lighting another cigarette, "but we can't manage the way things are. So I was wondering if maybe you could keep the baby . . . just till we get back on our feet."

Amana nodded without speaking.

"Just for a little while, Mama. Just so Jamie can get a job. He's got this notion of working in rodeo. Y'know, the prize money is good. And then, Mama, when we're

back on our feet, we can buy a nice little house some
where and settle down, and then *all* of us can live together again!"

"Yes . . . yes," Amana murmured in a dry voice,
sitting down and letting her wrinkled brown hands lie
lifelessly in her lap.

"Don't think I don't care about the baby," Jemina
said, taking him from Amana's back and balancing him
on her arm. She began to cry again. "I know you think
I'm wrong to leave him! But Mama, we can't stay here
in Fort Benton and let Jamie go off alone! I can't do
that, Mama, or he'll never come back, and then where
will I be!"

Amana smiled weakly as she got up. "Don't cry anymore," she said as she placed her palms upon Jemina's
head. "Don't cry. I will keep this child. I will raise him,
and when he is a man he will make things of beauty,
and you will be proud of him."

Jemina brightened. "Would you really, Mama!" she
said. "You don't think Amalia will mind about the baby,
do you?"

"No . . ." Amana murmured while she continued
to gaze at her daughter.

"You're a sweetheart, Mama," Jemina said, kissing
her mother and placing Reno in her arms. "And Mama,"
she said softly, "I want Reno to grow up to be a regular
little boy. I want him to have friends and to be happy.
He needs to learn how to be an American. Do you
know what I mean, Mama?"

Amana stood by the window with Reno in her arms

and stared down the highway that ran out into brown barren fields that had once sung with long twisting sweet-grass.

"Yes . . ." Amana whispered, "I know what you mean, Jemina. I know what you mean."

*　　*　　*

In the winter of the dust storms, Mr. Fuller died of a stroke.

Amalia was never the same after his death. She was older and bleaker than she had ever been in all the years Amana had known her.

Mr. Fuller's attorney said it was a poor investment to have a restaurant in such a rundown part of town. The buildings in the neighborhood had gotten shabby and dilapidated as families moved out one by one. Factories took over the empty houses and converted them into workshops filled with miserable people who worked from morning till night.

Mr. Fuller left Amalia and Amana a small sum of money as well as his business. Things being what they were, they decided to sell the restaurant.

Amana sent Jamie and Jemina five dollars once a month from the money Mr. Fuller had left her. She had put most of her savings into an automobile for Jamie, because he couldn't be in the rodeo without it. Amana had sent the money, and Jamie had bought an old pickup truck that he and Jemina lived out of when they were on the road.

There weren't any postcards from Jamie and Jemina anymore. And Amana saw them for only a few days during the winter, when they drove to Fort Benton to see Reno.

Reno was a big boy now. He had lived at Chez Amalia for seven years. He bullied the alley cats that had taken up residency in the parlor, and he flirted with the women of the house to get his way. Everyone adored Reno. Amana loved him too, but he had not brought back the good days for which she longed.

"Come . . . *aih, o-ke-nik-so-koo-wa* . . . come and say hello, my little son," Amana would call to Reno. But he would skip away with a wide smile that reminded her of Jean-Pierre Bonneville. The music of the gramophone had entranced Reno from the day he could walk. He sought the music, smiling his sweet smile; turning awkwardly among the dancing women; bowing to their applause, full of delight. He spent his days talking English with the women of the house. But he would not speak Blackfeet.

"Come along with us, Reno," the girls of the house would call to him. And then they would wrap themselves in blankets and sprawl out on the parlor rug, listening to the radio with their faces full of concern for the adventures of the hero called Jack Armstrong.

Reno whirled to the music. And he made a fuss if he didn't get his way.

On his seventh birthday Jamie and Jemina came home to Chez Amalia for a visit.

"Oh, what a big fellow you are!" Jamie exclaimed.

"Soon," Amana said, "he will be as tall as his father!"

Bang! Bang!

Reno lunged under the parlor table and fired the cap gun his father had given him for his birthday.

"How many did you shoot?" his father asked.

"I got ten of them!" Reno shouted excitedly, scrambling out from under the table and leaping into his father's arms. "I got ten of them Indians!"

Amana and Jamie looked at one another in astonishment.

"Reno . . . Reno!" Jamie scolded gently as he held his son's face in his hands and gazed into the boy's eyes. "What are you saying?"

"I really did! I got ten. I really shot ten of them Indians right in the head!"

"*Aih,*" Amana murmured. "He doesn't know what he is saying. It's all those crazy stories he hears on the radio!"

Reno grew taller. On Saturdays he cleaned the front yard for twenty-five cents and saved the quarters in a canning jar that Amana gave him.

"*Neets-so-pooks-see* . . . one dollar," Amana repeated slowly again and again. But Reno ignored the words as he methodically counted his coins.

"*Neets-so-pooks-see,*" Amana repeated.

"One dollar, two dollars . . ." Reno said defiantly.

Despite Amana's efforts to teach Reno some of the values of Indian life, he ignored the lessons. He was becoming just what his mother wanted him to be: an American boy.

Amana and Amalia watched strangers flood into Fort Benton and stampede across the land, searching for gold.

But there was no gold. The strangers did not become rich. They became disillusioned. Amana and Amalia sat on the porch and watched as the newcomers built houses and took over the old ranches and broke them up into tiny farms. And then factories began to crowd in among the houses and the air became gray. Starving stray dogs wandered the alleys and wailed.

"We are alone," Amana murmured to her old friend. "There is no one left but the two of us. How lonely the world has become."

"*Alors . . .* " Amalia sighed, reaching over to touch her friend's wrinkled hand.

"*Aih*, our friends have vanished. And what remains for us? Jemina is lost in dreams that are too small to come true. And Jamie," Amana moaned, "he wants to please a wife who cannot be pleased. Now even their child is lost. And soon there will be no one left but you and me."

And Amalia and Amana quietly wept.

Then Amalia wiped away her tears. "*Ma chère*, let us count the blessings. Life is good. And it has been long. We are old, but still we are here, my friend. It is a miracle, *ma chère*, that we have survived all the bad days and that we are here with one another. That is the miracle, *ma chère*! At least we will always have one another!"

They smiled at each other and said good night. Amalia turned out the lamps of Chez Amalia. Amana crept into Reno's room and smiled down upon the child and chanted softly. Then she went to bed.

But Amana could not sleep. She sat up in the darkness. Her chest ached and she could not catch her breath. In the darkness she tried to dream herself back into existence for yet another day. But living in a world without her own people was more terrible than not existing at all. In the darkness she summoned her sister, SoodaWa, and her husband, Far Away Son; she kissed her old friend Yellow Bird Woman; and she saw the grandmothers crouching patiently in the corner waiting for the day when the lost world would be found once again.

A frail lavender glow crept through Amana's window. The milk wagon brought bottles to people who did not live with cows anymore. The butcher hung meat in his window for those who did not know how to hunt. The factories lurched into motion and spoiled the morning with their clamor.

The house was utterly silent. The pain in Amana's chest spoke to her like an enemy. It frightened her. Each time she attempted to lie down on her buffalo robe, she felt her heart throb, and a terrible panic flooded her.

Suddenly she sat up and cried out. She had seen the door slowly open. Standing there in the dim lavender light of morning was a huge white owl.

Amana stumbled to her feet.

The light coming through the window turned yellow and an automobile backfired in the distance. The owl had vanished.

Quickly, Amana dressed and hurried downstairs. The parlor was dark, so she opened the velvet drapes and sat waiting for the women to come downstairs, laughing and talking and sending away Amana's terrible nightmare.

She waited a long time, until gradually her eyes dimmed from fatigue and she fell asleep.

When the sound of voices awakened Amana, she discovered that the women were already having breakfast in the large kitchen.

"Ah, there you are, Amana," Adella said. "We were just wondering when you and Amalia would be coming down."

Amana drew her fingers to her temples with the feeling that she had been struck hard against the head. For a moment she reeled, and then she leaned heavily against the door.

"Where is Amalia? Isn't she here with you?" she asked desperately.

"Why no. We thought . . ."

Amana cried out, and her voice rattled along behind her as she swung around and rushed upstairs to her friend's bedroom. The door was unlocked, and when Amana peered through the dimness at Amalia, she saw her on the bed with her arms widely spread and a broad contented smile on her face.

"My goodness, but you gave us a fright." Amana sighed. "Do you know what time of day it is?" Amana exclaimed as she raised the blinds.

There was no response.

She turned back toward the bed, and in the streaming

daylight she could see a great wind rise and vanish into the land.

"*E-spoom-mo-kin-on!* . . . Help us!" she screamed, covering her head and groaning as she fell to her knees beside the bed. "*E-spoom-mo-kin-on!* Amalia is dead!"

*　　*　　*

At dusk Amana went quietly down the stairs and locked the door of Chez Amalia. Then, as the women wept in the parlor, Amana went back to her old friend's bedroom. Deliberately, she hacked off her long, gray hair and painted her face white, and she began to chant. And when at last Sun had withdrawn from the sky, she gently wrapped the body of Amalia in a quilt, and she lay down beside her and she wept. Once again, Amana was truly alone.

FIVE

That winter Chez Amalia was sold.

The workmen came with their sledgehammers and sent up a cloud of dust as they broke the windows and the walls of the house. And when the debris and dust cleared away, there was nothing left but the brown earth.

After the terrible little funeral, the weeping women of Chez Amalia went away, vanishing into the crowds of Fort Benton, into railroad stations, into the streets. Adella wept bitterly as she said farewell.

Amana slowly put her possessions into a laundry bag and loaded it into Jamie Ghost Horse's pickup truck. And then she climbed in after it, and as the truck hurtled through endless miles, she huddled against the wind and embraced Reno and stared blankly into the alien landscapes she discovered day by day, a wide world that had once belonged to her people, a land she no longer recognized.

Salinas. Calgary. Pendleton. Cheyenne. Season after season Amana traveled with Reno and Jamie and Jemina on the powwow circuit. She clutched Reno by the hand, needing his protection as much as he needed hers. They sat in the bleachers in the midst of great crowds. The men shouted and fought and laughed and cursed.

And then suddenly all of them would bellow so that the earth shook.

The bull came thundering into the ring, stomping and blowing and flashing his wild eyes. Amana hugged Reno to her side and groaned as she looked into the face of the great, furious animal wheeling and tossing, trying to shake the rider from his back.

"What have they done to that animal to make him so crazy?" she cried.

Amana cowered when the rider plummeted to the ground and the bull surged forward in proud wide circles, with his great yellow head turning smartly from side to side.

The horses in the chutes danced. The cowboys swaggered and puffed on their black stogies. The clowns stumbled into the ring, waving checkered tablecloths at the bull, hooting and frolicking.

Then the chute opened and another bull with a man clinging to his back came bucking and leaping out into the ring. Amana could not watch anymore. She pulled Reno away and walked back to the truck.

"You shouldn't be watching such things, Reno. It's not good." Amana sighed and climbed into the back of the pickup.

"There's no harm in it, Grandma."

Amana muttered to herself as she set up a bucket of potatoes. "Grown people!" she snapped. "People with nothing to do with themselves! When I was a girl, people who mistreated animals would have been shamed. Once those poor beasts were mighty and strong."

Reno laughed. "It's a whole lot harder on the cowboy than it is on the bulls!" he said.

Amana cut off a big slice of the firm white meat of a potato and crunched upon it loudly.

"Come here, you young fox! Get a knife and start peeling. And after you get done with that, you'd best break up some more of the lettuce flats and build a nice big fire next to the truck, so I can start cooking our dinner."

"What I like," Reno was saying as he put more wood under the big black kettle, "what I like the most is bareback riding. Now that's really something, Grandma. You see, it's like bronco riding, but there's no saddle. You get on this bronco, y'see, sitting on nothing but this little pad made out of leather, and then you hang on for dear life with one hand, with your feet way out in front of you and your arm up in the air! No stirrups! No reins! Just a little piece of leather that's part of the rigging to hold on to! That's really something, Grandma!"

The sky was already getting dark when the voice on the public-address system announced the prizewinners. Disappointment filled Reno's face.

"Geez, he didn't win *anything*! Jamie just can't win for losing."

"Hush! Don't talk about your father like that."

"But that's what Mom always says."

"Your father does the best he can," Amana whispered.

Reno turned away and watched as the rodeo crowd started dispersing. A breeze came up and stirred Amana's little fire. The pickup trucks backfired, and the men shouted and laughed. Beer cans popped, and every now and again somebody let out a whoop or fired a rifle into the air.

Jemina walked slowly into the firelight, weary and dusty, with a deep frown on her face. She sat down heavily on an oil drum and stared into the flames without speaking. Amana pulled the kettle away from the coals. Reno stayed close to his grandmother and looked expectantly into the darkness for his father. All around them the encampment of pickups and tents glowed with many campfires.

They waited a long time. The men were still laughing and belching loudly somewhere out in the darkness. But Jamie did not come home.

Jemina got up and stared out into the darkness. "Go ahead and serve the dinner," she said at last.

*   *   *

That July they were back in Calgary. And after the rodeo they drove down into Montana. On their way Amana wanted Jamie to stop at the Blood reservation.

"Listen, Mama," Jemina insisted. "There aren't going to be any of your old friends around. That was years ago! Let's just go back to the highway and get going."

But Amana insisted that they stop at the agency office.

"Would you stop humoring her," Jemina snapped at Jamie when he pulled up in front of the tribal headquarters. "Isn't it bad enough without having to come all the way out here in the middle of nowhere!"

Amana laboriously climbed down from the truck and walked on unsteady legs toward the office.

When she returned, her face was drawn and she was breathing heavily. *"Aih,"* she groaned, climbing into the back of the pickup and sitting down on the blanket as she looked up into the sky with a little moan of pain. *"Aih."*

No one was left. No one remembered Amana. No one remembered the names of friends and relatives. There were no stories of the woman who had once been a warrior. All the legends had been forgotten. Even the memory of Far Away Son had vanished.

The people in the tribal office wore black suits. They looked at Amana as if she were an intruder. Their brown faces were the same as hers. Their words were in the same language. But they looked at her as if she did not belong among them anymore, as if she did not exist.

* * *

Night has come. A small fire burns in the pit of the medicine lodge. Cook fires smoulder in the arbor. But the big fire in the center of the ceremonial circle is where the great long flames leap skyward.

A group of singers starts to chant. Into the circle from the east dance five figures, swaying, posturing, twisting their arms in the firelight. Four of the dancers are masked in black. Each wears a black shirt and leggings of buckskin. In the hands of each dancer is a broad wooden sword.

The lone, fifth figure is painted white. He shines in the dark. Tied to his belt is a cowbell that clangs as he stomps and prances, making five circles around the great fire. Then the dancers begin to charge directly into the massive flames, thrusting their swords at each other and at the people standing silently in the darkness around them.

Reno sits with his mother in front of the truck, listening to the radio.

Amana is sitting on the ground, talking to some Apache women who came to the fair to sell jewelry and to see their old friends—to gossip and to laugh. They are not Amana's people, but they are old and they are Indians, and Amana is glad to be with them.

The Dance of the Mountain Spirits ends and the ceremonial dancers leave the arena. Now the head drum announces a round dance, and all the old people chatter and giggle merrily and stagger to their feet. They make a big circle and then, as the drum begins and the chanting soars, the circle moves around the great bonfire while all the dark faces are smiling. It is midnight before the round dance breaks up and small groups of people begin a back-and-forth dance. The lines sway forward and back, forward and back as the music throbs and the strong, clear voice of the singer raises everyone to a place of such strength and beauty that they weep and laugh as they sway forward and back, forward and back. Then lavender streaks of dawn begin to lighten the sky.

Amana gasps as she pants for breath and laughs with her friends. The camp is quiet now except for the whispers of the elders who have danced all night and are only now shuffling toward their beds.

"Good night . . . good night," Amana murmurs as she walks slowly toward the pickup truck.

Suddenly Amana lurches to the side and everything goes black. Her heart is pounding, and she sinks to her hands and knees in order to keep from fainting. The ground is damp and the dawn is humming in the grass. She can hear it. Somewhere a huge diesel truck bays into the silence. Then Amana swallows carefully and chants to herself for comfort as she tries to stand up.

"I thought . . . I thought I saw something," she whispers to herself as she carefully picks her way toward the truck on tottering feet.

Jamie is passed out on the front seat. Jemina and Reno are curled up in the back.

"*Aib*, I thought I saw an animal," Amana murmurs as she unfolds her blanket and, panting and blinking her eyes, lies down slowly. . . .

"I thought I saw a fox. . . ."

*   *   *

At the trading post of Aljato, Utah, there are two antique gas pumps, a masonry ruin, a couple of one-prop air taxis in the midst of a sprawling red desert, and a few clouds of dust.

The airplanes fascinate Reno. He circles them cautiously, staring at their rusty mechanical guts that hang out, dripping oil. The planes stand in the sunlit desert like rusty, wounded birds.

The summer day buzzes with flies and then suddenly lapses into silence.

Except for a few scrubby mesquites the land is as flat and bleak as the cloudless white sky above it.

The emptiness rings in Amana's ears.

Two white settlers run the trading post, the oldest business in the region. Their screen door bangs as a big Navajo man, his hair tied back in a queue and his head topped by a big black unblocked hat, comes in for his mail and a plug of tobacco, while his woman, in a long skirt and a blanket, sits in the wagon with the children bobbing around her like corks in a pond.

Jemina shakes her head disapprovingly as she stares at the Navajo family.

"Don't stare," Amana whispers.

But Jemina is not concerned with being polite. "I can understand dressing up for a powwow, but I think it's ridiculous to dress like that in this day and age!" she says.

She turns to Reno. "What's taking your father so long? Reno, honey, you go on inside and hurry him up. That man can't even buy four Cokes without taking all day about it!"

Amana climbs down from the truck. The sun is hot, and she is puffing and gasping as she opens the big black umbrella Jamie bought for her and squats down in its shade.

"Y'know, Mama, you're not looking yourself," Jemina says. "You okay?"

Amana tosses her head and huffs, *"Aih!"*

"It's about time!" Jemina calls as Jamie comes out of the trading post with Reno.

Jamie is drunk. He stumbles as he comes out the screen door, balancing the Coke bottles and grinning.

Jamie's boots are cracked and bent up in the toes. His jeans are baggy at the knees. He still has his wide silver buckle, but now his belly hangs over and obscures it. The Stetson that Amana bought him for his birthday is stained with sweat and the pheasant-feather band has disappeared.

"It's so hot out here I thought Amana was going to faint. Whatever took so long, Jamie?"

He ignores his wife's question as he stumbles behind the shed.

Amana silently watches a trail of dust that is forming far out in the desert as a truck and a couple of station wagons rumble toward the trading post.

Eventually the vehicles pull into the parking area, and the proprietor ambles from the trading post, taking his time. He pulls the hose from one of the pumps and says, without looking at the white visitors, "How much do you want and where do you want it?"

Jemina turns away and takes Reno by the shoulder, walking with him to the other side of their truck. She gives him her empty Coke bottle.

"Now, honey, you get all the bottles, y'hear, and take them back for the deposit. You can keep the money. And if you got to do anything, you just hurry on in back of the shed right now and get it taken care of.

So hurry along, Reno, 'cause we got to get going as soon as your father gets back."

Reno hesitates, peering over the fender at the white people who are talking loudly.

"Never you mind about them," Jemina says.

Suddenly Jamie comes stumbling around the truck toward Jemina, ducking down and muttering, "Jesus Christ, let's get the hell out of here!"

"What's the matter?" Jemina exclaims. "You dally around and now you're in such a hurry Amana can't even finish her Coke!"

"Come on . . . come on! Let's get moving! We gotta get out of here right now!"

"What's going on?" Jemina asks suspiciously. "Are you in some sort of trouble with those white people?"

At that moment a man with a foreign accent cries out and rushes toward Jamie.

"*Malista! Malista!* My Gods, it's you, Jamie!" the man exclaims.

When Jamie sees a smile on the man's face he shyly nods his head.

"Yes, yes, it's you for sure. My old friend. My very dear friend, I can't believe I find you way out here! Don't you recognize me? It's Alexander! Alexander Milas from Athens! *The great Milas Family Troupe of Aerialists!*"

*   *   *

"So anyway," Alexander Milas was saying as they had lunch at a cafe in Window Rock, "I stayed behind in America when my family went back to Greece. And for maybe ten years I've been producing shows. Putting together all kinds of shows and dreaming up crazy schemes!"

"And why have you come to Utah, Mr. Milas?" Jemina asked.

"Please, you will all call me Alex. That's what they call me in America! Alex the Great!" He laughed loudly. "To tell the truth, we came out here about a month ago to finish a little project. We've been looking to put together a serial for RKO Studios. There's a lot of money in serials."

Jemina's excitement filled her face. "Well, Alex, if you need somebody who can do every kind of stunt on horseback, don't forget your friend Jamie!" she exclaimed. "Because he's really something! Did you know that he's a big star in the rodeo? Well, he is . . . and he's done just about everything you can do on a horse when it comes to fancy trick riding!"

"You old son of a gun." Alexander Milas laughed as he stood up and embraced Jamie. "So you went and made a big success of yourself!"

Jamie shook his head with confusion and glanced at Jemina. Before he could respond, she said, "Well, Alex, since the Depression it's been a bit hard on us. And there's no use pretending that we haven't been down on our luck. But there's nobody more willing than Jamie to make a dollar and do something exciting with his life!"

"That so . . . that so," Alexander Milas mused as

he gazed at Jamie. "Well, I just might be able to use you. How would you like to work for me? I could sure use some help with these Indians," he added. "It's like pulling teeth to get them to sit still while we photograph them!"

Jemina laughed with delight as Jamie and Alexander shook hands.

That winter the radio announced the bombing of Pearl Harbor.

*   *   *

Amana sat in the shadows of the walnut grove that surrounded the little guest house on Alexander Milas' estate in the San Fernando Valley. This had been the family's home since Jamie had become a stuntman.

She closed her eyes and sighed. The dizziness had gotten worse. At night sometimes she could not catch her breath. When Amana awakened in the morning, she didn't know for certain where she was. Sometimes her legs ached so badly that she couldn't get out of bed. And sometimes she got dizzy when she sat up and called out for Jamie.

But he had run off. One night he had gotten crazy with whiskey and had hit Jemina, and then Alexander Milas had come rushing into the house and there had been a big argument. And Jamie had run off.

"I'm not being your goddamn Indian anymore!" Jamie had shouted at Alexander. "And you just stay away from my wife or I'm gonna break both of your legs!"

There was a great deal of shouting. And Jamie was

so drunk he didn't know what he was doing or saying. Then he slapped Jemina, and suddenly he started crying and he ran out to his car and drove off like a madman.

That was the last time Amana had seen Jamie. And she missed him terribly.

One morning, about a week later, Amana heard Jamie's pickup coming up the long driveway.

"*Aih* . . . it's Jamie!" she cried happily. And she rushed out to greet him.

"No . . . no, Amana . . . don't look at me," he pleaded, hiding his bruised face behind his hands. "I've been scrapping and drinking hard and raising a lot of hell. I don't want you looking at me. I just came back to see Jemina."

Amana embraced Jamie and begged him to sit down and rest, before he did something he would regret. But then Jemina shouted down from her bedroom window: "Tell him to get out of here or I'll call the police!"

Jamie roared with pain and anger and stumbled into the house, shouting and pushing furniture over as he raced upstairs.

Amana cried out and grabbed Reno, pulling him out the door, running as fast as she could to Alexander Milas' house and banging desperately at his door.

"Jamie is here! Don't go down to the guest house, Mr. Milas. Stay here with Reno and don't go down there no matter what happens!"

*　　*　　*

Amana sat up all night while Reno slept on Alexander's couch. She went out on the porch several times during the night and peered through the leaves toward the guest house, but there was no sound.

In the morning when she crept back, she found Jemina in bed crying.

"I never want to see him again!" she wept when Amana tried to comfort her.

Amana stroked her daughter's tangled hair and stared down at Jamie, who was passed out on the floor by the bed.

"What am I going to do, Mama?" she wept. "He hurt me. He hurt me, Mama."

"Forgive him . . . you must forgive him," Amana sang as she rocked her daughter in her arms. Then the song dried up in her throat and her mouth was full of dust and despair.

S I X

Summer flooded the meadow with yellow flowers.

It was that summer that Sitko was born. Amana sat in the waiting room of the hospital, withdrawn and nervous, peering at the nurses, whose chalky faces were full of indifference. Amana huddled in a corner, waiting for Jemina's baby to be born in this terrifying place of white walls and white halls and white nurses.

It was on that white summer day that Sitko was born. And when Amana saw him for the first time, it was like seeing a meadow of yellow flowers. He was so beautiful! His thick black hair and deep brown skin were so lovely that Amana laughed with surprise. The child had the eyes of her sister, SoodaWa. Amana gazed at him in astonishment. He was surely a good memory born again.

Amana took this new child into her arms. "Napi!" she exclaimed, closing her warm body around the infant. "Is this the child I have been waiting for? Is this the boy who will keep our heritage alive?"

The tongues of ten thousand meadow flowers survived in Amana's mind. And there was also within her a place where Napi still flowed as a silver river. In her right hand she held the Sun and in her left hand the Moon. And upon her breasts were the wide plains and the high mountains, the valleys of the lizards and the lakes where the water slept in its own blue dream.

All this was the heritage of the new child.

When Jemina was ready to leave the hospital, Amana would not let anyone else hold Sitko. Once she had lost Reno to the women of Chez Amalia, but she would not lose Sitko. She murmured in his ears. She tucked him into her life and would not let him go.

The summer passed. Jemina and Jamie were rarely home together. He worked a few days a month as a stuntman at the studio, and the rest of the time he ran off with his drinking buddies. Jemina lived her own life, traveling and going out with Alexander Milas. Then one day Jamie came home and quietly waited for Jemina to return from a party. He insisted that she sit down and listen to what he had to say. "I'm sending the children away."

Jemina did not respond.

"I'm sending Amana and the boys to live on the reservation. I want them to get out of this house. I wrote a letter for Amana. She asked the tribal chairman for a house in her father's land, where the children can grow up and learn the ancient ways of their grandmother."

Jemina started to object, but Jamie made a gesture so filled with rage that she drew a breath and walked from the room.

Amana awaited a response to her request, but when the letter finally arrived, it was only a formal sentence or two, explaining that there was no record of Amana's family on the tribal logs, and the tribe could not provide housing for nonenrolled Indians.

Amana turned away when Jamie read the letter to her. She gazed out the window and did not dare speak.

"It doesn't matter," Jamie gently said as he embraced her. "I promised to send you away from here, and I'll keep that promise. I'll find a house for you in Montana."

Amana hugged Jamie and nodded to him with tears in her eyes.

"Besides," he said with a dry laugh, "I've got to get the children away from this house and all the craziness that's been going on here!"

"But, Jamie, can't Jemina go with us?" Amana whispered.

"No!" he exclaimed, rage welling up abruptly and violently. It frightened Amana to realize how far apart Jamie and Jemina had come.

Amana grasped Jamie's hand. "Don't be angry," she whispered. "Jemina is a good woman. . . . Please don't be angry with her. It frightens me to see you so angry," Amana said.

"I promised you a house," he repeated softly to Amana. "Jemina's not telling me where to raise my kids!"

Jamie kept his promise, and by the next spring, Amana and the boys had moved to the northern plains.

It was a handsome region. The creeks were full of birds. They flitted in the shallow water, chirping and tossing spray. Then they muddled in the warm sandbank, raising tiny clouds of dust as they dried themselves.

The Blackfeet lands reached into the sky at the foot of the Rocky Mountains. It was a good place, where there was still deep silence and much power in the rocks. A place where Napi's morning song could be heard by all the animals and people.

Amana breathed the sweet mountain air that she had so much loved as a young woman. She was contented at last. The bad days were surely over. Her two grand-children were a couple of puppies—sniffing and exploring the land, frolicking in the grass, and running headlong through the rooms of the house.

It was a very good time.

The old people came in the evening to sing with Amana. Joe White Calf and his handsome Nez Percé wife, Henrietta, became Amana's friends; they watched after the baby or sat over the fire long into the night while they recalled the long-ago days.

Then, when her friends went home, Amana would creep into the boys' bedroom and sit next to Reno, gazing down at him.

He smiled up at her.

"Why aren't you asleep, Reno?" she whispered.

"When is Mother coming to see us?" Reno asked.

"Jamie and your mother have gone to Death Valley to work," Amana said.

"I don't see why Mama's always got to be going away," the child complained.

"Jamie has to work so we can have this nice house."

"Well, why can't he work around here like all the other fathers?"

"Because your father works in the motion pictures, and you should be proud of that," Amana whispered patiently. "You know that he has to go wherever they need him. That's his job, Reno."

"But why can't I go with them so they can keep me company?"

"You have got the whole countryside to keep you company," Amana said with a smile. "You've got five million birds and deer and elk. And you've got the Rocky Mountains as well. Isn't that enough company?"

Reno smiled and Amana chuckled softly.

"You mean I own all that?" Reno laughed.

"Now hush or you'll wake your brother," Amana said with a good-natured nod of her head. "It's time for you to be asleep."

Reno hugged his grandmother and said good night. And then, with a smile on his lips, he fell asleep under her gaze.

It was a good time for Amana at last.

*   *   *

The darkness was filled with the sounds of crickets. The brothers entertained each other in front of the fireplace, and Amana dozed contentedly, opening her eyes now and again to look at the two golden children playing in the firelight. One boy was as tall and handsome as his father, while the other—little Sitko—was as fragile and delicate as a doe, with beautiful long black hair cascading over his shoulders.

Every night when Amana came into the boys' room to say good night, she would tell them stories. Reno was impatient with the old legends, but Sitko listened to every word, lying back on his pillow with his large eyes fixed on Amana.

"Now," she whispered, "it is time to close your eyes. Yes, close them tight. *Kin-yok* . . . that's it, just look at the dark place behind your eyes and listen to what Grandmother Amana tells you. *Ke-da-yo-toks-pa?* . . . Do you hear what I say?"

Then Amana prayed for everything in the world. She prayed for the four-legged people and for the family of Jamie Ghost Horse, and for the *na-pe-koo-wan* . . . the white people.

"Now you must go to sleep," she murmured, "because soon it will be a special day."

Sitko sat up excitedly, exclaiming, "What is it? Tell us! What is the special day?"

"I will tell you. Soon we go to the Beaver Ceremony!"

Sitko's eyes grew large.

"*Aih!*" he whispered. "It will be the first time that I am old enough to go to the ceremony!"

Then the child turned over and pressed his head to the pillow and smiled to himself as he watched Amana slowly lower her body to the old buffalo robe on the floor next to the children's beds.

"Oh!" Reno said sadly. "I thought that Jamie and Mother were finally coming to see us."

"They will come home for the ceremony," Amana

assured him. "But now it is time for dreaming," Amana whispered in the darkness.

* * *

But Jamie and Jemina did not return for the Beaver Ceremony. Reno was so disappointed that he wandered away from the house after breakfast.

"Don't be gone long," Amana called to him. "We must be ready to leave as soon as the White Calfs get here."

Reno muttered a response as he vanished into the woods.

"Poor child," Amana murmured as she fixed Sitko's hair in long braids.

When Amana had finished, Joe and Henrietta White Calf banged on the screen door and invited themselves in for coffee.

Amana was comforted by the sight of her good friends. Joe had a new suit and his hair was freshly clipped. And Henrietta was wearing her best necklace with a large beaded pendant.

"Sit down. Please, sit down and be comfortable," Amana said. "I have a fresh pot of coffee ready!"

Amana served her guests and embraced Sitko, showing him off and feeling proud when Joe White Calf said, "Now isn't he the best-looking young Indian on the reservation!"

When at last it was time to get into Joe's station wagon and leave for the house where the ceremony was to be held, Amana could not find Reno. She called and called for him, but he did not answer.

"What's the matter with that boy?" she murmured to the White Calfs.

They glanced uncomfortably at one another as Amana called for Reno again and again. Then they stood very quietly as Amana took out a handkerchief and blew her nose to hide her tears.

They were already late for the ceremony, and finally they had to leave without Reno.

Sitko craned his neck, looking back at the house for some sign of his brother as the station wagon chugged into the puddles and down the narrow dirt road, but the meadow was motionless and the woods were silent. There was no sign of Reno.

It was so cold when they arrived at the ceremonial house that the children were still in their beds and only Mrs. Buffalo and her friend Mary Little Dog were busy in the kitchen, preparing big pots of food for the ritual feast. And when the youngsters of the house finally staggered into the kitchen, their mother told them to get dressed and to eat their breakfast hurriedly, for the guests were already arriving.

"You hear me?" she said. "We have lots of work to do, so eat up and get out from under foot, y'hear?"

Soon other people arrived, and it wasn't long before the house was overflowing with friends, quietly speaking Blackfeet.

Then the Beaver Ceremony began.

Sitko watched as the world of his people unfolded in the dimness. The Beaver Man, standing in the shadows, gradually sank to the floor. It was the signal. Instantly the drummers' fingers began to throb on their resounding instruments. Rattles answered the drums, turning the air of the room warm and alive. Amana closed her eyes. The shrill piping of the eagle-bone whistles pierced her heart with gladness and dread, so sacred was the Beaver Ceremony. Sitko drew close to Amana's body and heard her pulse ringing in his ears.

The walls faded away. The floor turned to animal skin. The ceiling flew into the endless sky. And the four drums spoke loudly.

As the pungent incense of sweetgrass rose, the Beaver Bundle came into its ancient place before the Beaver Man, and each male elder stood in the smoking, humming place as the air turned silver. Their bodies turned slowly around the circle, arms and heads moving, feet stepping soundlessly, dancing as the sacred pipe was passed and breathed into the spirit of each man.

Amana opened her eyes as the Beaver Bundle was gently unwrapped by the Beaver Chief. Now the chanting came up from the earth. Now the drums made their strong music. Now Sitko peered in astonishment as the Bundle disclosed itself, like a rose, opening out into the smoke and the singing, as the sacred objects were carefully lifted, one by one, and placed on the furs covering the floor.

An albino crow whose eyes were sealed with memory. The furs of powerful beings who dressed themselves as animals that people might not know them: beaver, otter, weasel, mink, marten, ermine. Their hissing, grunting, snarling voices joined the song. The fire turned purple and sparks fell like stars. And then suddenly . . . silence.

All heads turned. All eyes gazed downward. And slowly the Chief lifted from the Bundle four sacred buffalo stones.

The stones began to spin in his palms as the Chief held them. They began to glow and to sputter and to speak. And within each stone there was the bright yellow spark from which Napi, the Old Man who had made the world, had ignited the cosmos with the idea of being. And the speech of these buffalo stones was so intense and so loud that it rang in Sitko's ears until tears came into his eyes and he felt faint and clutched Amana lest he fall into the darkness.

Sitko could hear the talking of the stones and the chanting of the people as he rose to his feet and moved toward the Chief, feeling the old man's gentle fingers upon his face.

Sitko could feel Sun and Moon as the Chief painted his cheeks. He could feel the power of his people, and their many days filled his body when the Chief made the sign of Morning Star upon his forehead and blessed him with the gift of vision.

"This child shall see," he murmured fiercely. "This child shall have a vision in his fingertips!" the Chief proclaimed.

Amana wept with pride. She watched Sitko's body twist like smoke in the air as the Chief turned the boy into a hoop of fire that hung in the air. She chanted and she prayed as Sitko emerged from the fire and knelt before the Chief.

"Little one," the old man murmured as he painted Sitko's face, "you must learn to see truly so your vision can come to you and give you strength. You must learn to see in the night. You must learn to see with more than your eyes. You must find eyes in the shadows. You must learn to look at the world twice. First you must bring your eyes together in front so you can see each droplet of rain on the grass, so you can see the smoke rising from an anthill in the sunshine. Then you must learn to look again with your eyes at the very edge of what is visible. Now you must see dimly if you wish to see things that are dim—visions, mists, and cloud people, animals that hurry past you in the dark. You must learn to look at the world twice."

*　　*　　*

It was not until the next afternoon that Jemina finally arrived at the house, toting her suitcase.

"Where is your husband?" Amana asked.

"I don't know where he is! And what's more, I don't care!" Jemina said.

"These children have done nothing but ask me when you and Jamie were coming to see them. It will break Reno's heart not seeing his father."

"Mama, that's not my fault. He's impossible!" Jemina said forlornly as she dropped her suitcase and flopped into a chair. "Either he's fighting with me or he's drunk somewhere. It's gotten so bad, Mama, that he can't get work anymore. Nobody can rely on him anymore. He's one of the best stuntmen in Hollywood, but he can't stay sober long enough to make a living! It's just terrible, Mama. I don't know what I'm going to do," Jemina complained as she lit a cigarette. "Even Alex has lost patience with his craziness. Even a friend can take just so much!"

"What kind of a friend is this Mr. Milas, anyway?" Amana asked with a dark expression filling her eyes. "This Mr. Milas is too busy chasing the women to be anybody's friend!"

"*Miller*, Mama! Not Milas! His name is Miller. He changed his name to Miller."

"What do you have to do with this man? Why is he always standing between you and your husband?"

"What do you mean by that, Mama? You act like it's a crime for me to have friends. We owe absolutely everything to Alex! I'll tell you something, Mama—if it weren't for Alex Miller, I don't know how we would have managed. He doesn't charge us rent for the guest house, and he even pays for this place most of the time. Jamie may have promised you this place, but it's Alex who has to pay for it. He even had to pay Jamie's bar tab last month. I'll tell you, he cares more about these kids than Jamie does!"

"Don't tell me about Jamie's love for his children!" Amana said. "He would die before he would let anything happen to Reno and Sitko. Such talk!" Amana muttered as she glanced at the boys and softly said, "You two do as your grandmother tells you. Go outside till dinner. I must talk to your mother."

"Mama, it's not my fault. You always take Jamie's side. Should I just curl up and die because I married a drunk? You and Amalia couldn't get me married fast enough. I was only sixteen years old, Mama! What did I know about living with a drunk?"

"*Aih*, but he wasn't a drunk when you married him. He was good-looking and strong and he had a mind of his own!"

"Well, I'll tell you one thing, Mama. That's not what he is today. And I'm not going to wait around for him. That's what I've come all the way up here to tell you. This is the end, Mama! I mean it! This is really the end. I'm taking the children and I'm leaving Jamie for good, Mama! I'm going to an attorney and I'm getting legal custody of the kids so I can raise them properly. All the time I've done what you wanted and I've forgiven Jamie. But this time it's finished!"

"You can't take a man's children away from him," Amana pleaded. "You cannot just take away Jamie's boys!"

"It's already decided, Mama. There's nothing you can say to talk me out of it. I've listened to you and I've done what you've told me to do time and again. But this time I'm finished. I told Jamie if he didn't come here to see the kids, he might just as well forget about coming back home. He just laughed in my face and walked off with his friends. So don't tell me about being a good wife! I'm finished being a good wife! There's nothing more to say about it!''

At dinner Jemina didn't eat. She sat in front of a cup of coffee and stirred it mechanically with a sad look on her face.

After the meal Amana braided Sitko's hair, tying it with strips of red cloth. All the while Jemina gazed into the air and smoked cigarette after cigarette.

"I just don't know what to do," Jemina whimpered again and again. "Mama, I just don't know what to do."

"Talk to him. He's a reasonable man. Just try to talk to him, Jemina."

"Oh, Mama, I've talked to him a million times about his drinking."

"Let me talk to him, Jemina. Let me try talking to him!''

"Mama, you've talked to him a hundred times before and it didn't do a bit of good. A week later he was back on a drunk again, spending every dime we have and disappearing for days and weeks at a time. And he'll just do it again. He'll run off, and then when he comes back he'll be crazy with whiskey."

Reno had been quietly sitting at the table watching. "Papa's never coming back, is he?" he said.

"Never mind," Jemina said softly. "You're already a big fellow and everything is going to be fine for us. So you go on out when you've finished your dinner and see if you can get the old pickup started. 'Cause tomorrow morning first thing, we're going to pack our things and we're going back to California. Y'hear, honey, we're going right back home to your friends."

"You really mean it, Mom?" Reno exclaimed happily.

"Aih," groaned Amana. "What kind of a boy are you that you do not care about your father?" she wailed.

"Mama, just leave him alone. He's already so mixed up from all your talk that he doesn't know who his father is! So just leave Reno alone!"

"Aih," Amana continued deliberately as she gazed at Reno. "You can be happy that your father is gone forever, but your grandmother can see what you cannot see. *Aih!"* she wailed as she slowly nodded her head and a fierce blue light came into her eyes. "Be careful, Reno, because I see where you are going. You are walking into the den of the owls. There is nothing but sorrow . . . there is nothing but death and despair!"

Reno drew back in dread when he saw the blue light flash in his grandmother's eyes. He trembled as he saw white feathers falling through the air, tumbling down upon the head of Grandmother Amana. Reno gasped and turned away as an owl slowly took shape within the snarls of Amana's hair and blinked its great yellow eyes.

Then suddenly Jemina lit a cigarette, and in the flare of the match the vision disappeared.

* * *

At night Amana sat on Sitko's bed while Jemina read an old magazine. The little boy looked steadily at his grandmother, waiting for her to tell him a story. But Amana could not speak. She watched her daughter puffing relentlessly on a cigarette and flipping noisily through the pages of the magazine. Amana could not summon the stories of Napi on such a night as this; she could not find her way back into the place where the stories lived.

"Where's Reno off to, Mama?" Jemina asked without looking at her mother.

"He went in the truck." Amana murmured. "He went down to the junction," she whispered. "He went to get some beer for you."

"Why are you staring at me, Mama?" Jemina asked with deep discomfort. "Why are you always staring at me?"

Silently, Amana took Sitko by the hand and prepared him for bed. She closed the door behind them, and she sat with the child and rocked him in her arms.

"What's the matter, Grandma?" he asked.

"Nothing . . . nothing . . . nothing. Now you must close your eyes and go to sleep, because tomorrow when we get up, all of this will be gone forever. The meadow and the mountains and the trees. All of it will be gone, Sitko, because you are going back to California with your mother."

"But I can't go to sleep without a story," the child said. "Please," he pleaded, "tell me about when you had a gun and when you were the best shot in the whole Northwest Territory, Grandma!"

So Amana closed her eyes and searched in the dark for the long-ago days. And then, very slowly and in a strange, chanting voice, she told Sitko about the winter when she had been changed into a man by Grandfather Fox.

When she had finished her story, Sitko gazed up at her through sleepy eyes and grinned happily.

"These are the things I give to you, child," Amana whispered. "These memories of our people . . . these legends, these things of my life. These memories are the things that I give to you, Sitko."

Now he closed his eyes slowly.

"I give you life through many generations. Because it was here inside me that Napi placed the seeds of all the life of the earth. And I give you that life, Sitko. I give you the memories that fill each of us with time."

And then Amana wept as she rocked the child in her arms. Amana cried and wailed as her spirit rose, filling the little house and the meadow beyond the house with immense blue light.

"Aih," Amana chanted as she looked into the future. *"Aih!"* Amana wailed as she held the child high above the river of blood.

SEVEN

In the morning Henrietta White Calf came to comfort Amana. The two women sat on the porch in the cold breeze and nodded their heads in silence, staring off toward the mountains.

Jemina had taken the children away. They had been taken away to a boarding school.

And Amana had stood in the doorway holding back her grief until the car was out of sight. And then she screamed and she painted her face white and she hacked off her long white hair and fell to her knees.

In the night the sounds of her chanting filled the meadow. In the morning Henrietta White Calf came to comfort Amana.

"What are you thinking?" the woman asked Amana in a whisper.

Amana frowned, but she did not answer.

I am trying to recall who I am and where I came from and where I am going now that my life is over.

I am thinking of Jemina. I am thinking of her face.

That is what I am thinking. My mind is filled with Jemina and Jamie. But they are only the largest people in the darkness.

Beyond them are other people and other days.

I am remembering the first time I rode a horse. And I can see the smile of my sister, SoodaWa. Beneath every day of my life there is some fragile trace of the people I have known and loved. In the snow of every winter I have left some small sign of those I love. And the summers are still filled with the songs I sang and the Sun Dances and the drums and many yellow mornings.

I am thinking of these things as I go into my room and pull the old trunk from under the bed. I sing the old songs and weep with the memory of Sitko's frightened eyes as they took him away from me. And I am praying to Sun for courage.

I was a foolish woman who was given a great vision when I was young. I did not understand the power that had been given to me, and so it was taken away.

Here, in this little bundle containing the faded regalia of a warrior, are the only riches I have ever had. In this bundle there is a great gift that died because I was too foolish to understand its power.

Now, Sun, I give you this vow. Give me back little Sitko and I will build a lodge for you more handsome than any of those we made long ago in the days when the legends were still alive. Give me back the child so he can learn from the winters and the summers of my life, from the fragile traces of my people that remain beneath every day of the world! And I vow to build a fine lodge to you!

That is why I have taken out this sacred bundle. And that is why I am climbing into the willow and placing it upon the highest limb as a sacrifice to you. Now, Sun, give me back the child so our people may live in him!